Alpine
Dove

Alpine
Dove

by

Judy A. Crawford

BONNEVILLE BOOKS
Springville, Utah

ISBN: 978-1-55517-560-0

Published by Bonneville Books, an imprint of Cedar Fort, Inc.
2373 W. 700 S., Springville, UT, 84663
Distributed by Cedar Fort, Inc., www.cedarfort.com

LIBRARY OF CONGRESS CATALOGING-IN-PUBLICATION DATA

Crawford, Judy A. (Judy Ann)
Alpine dove / by Judy A. Crawford.
   p. cm.
ISBN 1-55517-560-0
1. Canadians--Europe--Fiction. 2. Abused wives--Fiction. 3.
Europe--Fiction. I. Title.
PS3553.R282 A78 2001
813'.54--dc21
                              2001003730

Typeset by Virginia Reeder
Cover design by Adam Ford
Cover design © 2001 by Lyle Mortimer
Printed in the United States of America

10 9 8 7 6 5 4 3 2

Printed on acid-free paper

Dedication

To my parents, my friends,
my siblings, and my six children
for their never-ending
encouragement and support.

Acknowledgments

I wish to express my gratitude for all those who believed in me and helped in any way to forward the completion of this novel. My family and friends have been a great support in overlooking my emotions as I put my whole self into telling this timely story.

I wish to acknowledge Ray Sheen and his wife Chris for editing the book and working with me until it told the story "just right."

Thank you to those who read and critiqued the book: Mary Nugent, Ellen Conrad, Tamra Echternacht, and Ray Sheen.

I especially thank Bryce Paton, Director of Communications of the Calgary Airport Authority, for spending his valuable time in showing me the workings of an international airport and in helping me find a realistic, exciting, and surprise ending to the European chase.

Foreword

Abuse in any form affects the victim for a lifetime. Without the support of caring, understanding, and patient people the healing process would never happen.

Hopefully *Alpine Dove* will encourage those in an abusive situation to take action before it is too late. At a time when the world prays for the cycle of abuse to be broken, may this story aid in that endeavor.

Chapter One

The nose of the plane lifted but it did nothing to raise Michelle Enger's spirits. She watched buildings and roads rush past the small window, miniaturize, then disappear under wisps and puffs of white cloud.

Michelle could see Max out of the corner of her eye twisting the corner of his thick black mustache as he read the emergency pamphlet from the pocket in front of him. Her grip on the arm rests slackened as the plane leveled and she realized her fingers ached. She took a deep breath trying to get her whole body to relax. A slight shake of her head and her downcast eyes were the only signs of discontent and these she hoped Max would not see. She was here, sitting beside him on a trip to Europe she had not wanted to take.

As if reading her thoughts, her husband turned to her, "We finally made it," he said without provocation. "There were times when I doubted our departure." He stuffed the magazine back into the pocket just as the flight attendant began her safety instructions.

Michelle cringed, trying to think of an appropriate response, but one did not come to mind so she focused on what the attendant was saying. Ignoring the instruction, as if it were not happening, Max leaned over Michelle to look out her window. "Too bad there's this cloud cover. We'll soon be over the ocean, and I always watch the ships and floating icebergs."

That's par for the course, Michelle thought. It's as cloudy as the heaviness in my heart. She caught a whiff of Max's after-shave as he sat back in his seat. The potency was nauseating.

Her silence made him leery. "You're not nervous, are you?" he asked tersely.

"No," she replied almost repentantly, her eyes on the silver wings that split the white fluffy clouds. "I just have a bit of a headache."

"From the change in air pressure," he volunteered emphatically. "It'll pass as soon as you get used to it." He laid his head back against the seat and closed his eyes.

Michelle kept her eyes staring out the window. Air pressure? she asked herself. I've never flown before. I've never left my children for more than a few days before. I'm embarrassed and almost afraid to be around you, and you tell me my head-ache is from the change in air pressure. Her rebellious thoughts continued angrily. I don't want to be here. I don't want to be here with you. She shuddered at her own anger, then tensed, afraid he would feel her aggression.

She needn't have worried. Max was breathing his hot breath in her ear, his voice a raspy whisper. "You're going to have a good time, wife. I'll see to that. Just imagine," he fingered her long brown hair, "our first night will be in the Hotel D'Azure in Paris. Aah, making love to you in grand Paree."

Michelle pulled away but turned to give him her usual phony smile. He didn't notice anything amiss; his thoughts were too far away.

A stewardess interrupted with a trolley of drinks. Max ordered a gin and tonic, but Michelle just shook her head. "Have a sherry," Max said, and again it sounded like an order.

"All right," she whispered.

After gulping his drink down in one long swallow, Max busied himself with a new book he had bought at the duty free shop in Toronto. Michelle set her glass on the table in front of her, her attention going to the marshmallow scenery outside her window. She was still nursing her drink long after their dinner arrived.

The seafood and steak meal were delicious and she turned to Max. "I wonder how they do such nice meals on an airplane?"

"Oh, speaking to me now are you?" he said with a sneer. Michelle felt herself withdraw. "I guess you've decided to enjoy this expensive delicacy I've paid for?"

"I only asked," she commented softly, the magic gone from the meal.

"Well, make sure you eat it. I intend to take full advantage of everything this month. It's the first time I've managed to get you away from the kids for any length of time." He shoved a large piece of meat into his mouth.

"Don't always bring up the children. They're as much yours as mine."

"Not hardly. I may have gotten you pregnant but none of them picked up any of my traits." Thank God, Michelle thought. "Well, maybe Sonja," Max added, fingering a piece of shrimp he finally stuck in his mouth. "She's tough enough to be mine."

"I don't believe you, Max. Do you think being tough is always the answer?"

"It gets me where I want to go."

"And how many toes do you step on?"

"Only those who are weak and need to be stepped on." His glare was icy, and Michelle knew she had gone too far. That's me, she told herself. A weak one. Turning back to her meal, her appetite totally gone, she could only pick at the food.

3

Noisily her husband finished his meal without speaking again.

Michelle was glad when Max's novel fell to his lap showing he had dozed off. Even in sleep his black hair and thick dark eyebrows gave him an austere look. Carefully she took her walkman from her carry-on bag, slipped in a tape and placed the headphones over her ears. Her movements were deliberate so as not to wake up Max. She had just begun to relax with the music when he pulled the headphones from her ear. "What are you doing with this?"

"Anna gave it to me. She thought I would enjoy the music while we were flying." Michelle's stomach tied in knots. If he knew it was the music Anna and Michelle had collected over the months, he would toss it out the window if he could.

"Well, you look stupid. Only teenagers wear earphones. Take them off!"

Michelle was angry but she put the walkman back into her bag and turned to the white brightness outside her window.

She must have dozed, for Max's loud laughter made her sit up. The plane was dark, and cartoons were lighting up a screen in front her. "Good! You're awake! You'll enjoy tonight's movie. It's 'Coach' with Whoopi Goldberg." He took hold of her hand. "I love movies in the dark."

Michelle tried not to stiffen in order to ignore Max's grip on her hand. She wished he would watch the movie and let her listen to the music on the walkman. She did not feel like laughing tonight. However, sitting in the dark and with the movements on the screen in front of her Michelle decided she didn't have much choice. She took the airline headphones out of their plastic bag and placed them on her head. Fortunately, she was able to get involved with the show and put some of her anxieties away. She couldn't help but laugh at Whoopi's antics. It was then she decided she would take these little escapes and use them to her advantage. Maybe she might even enjoy some

4

of the things she would do and see while on this trip. "That's my mother," Michelle could hear Sonja saying. "Optimistic at all times, even if it kills her." It really is the only way to survive Michelle said to herself, and this is one of those times when I need to make the most of my predicament or have a month of agony. Michelle slid down in her seat to watch the movie.

By the time it was over Max had slipped into a deep sleep. Michelle had long taken her hand from his and leaned back letting the hum of the engines lull her. As soon as her husband's breathing became deep and low, she carefully pulled out the walkman. Within seconds she felt herself relax and let her mind drift to her children.

Billy, at the age of twenty-two, had been away from home for four years now, graduated from college and was well known for his cooking skills. He may not have been as robust as his father, but he was dark like his father and had his father's green eyes. He was slight statured like his mother, and was very personable so did well as a chef at Alexandro's in Montreal. Billy didn't get many days off to come home, and that's the way he liked it. Max had hated it when Michelle called William, Billy. He thought it a sissy name. When Billy was born Max wanted to call him Wilhelm Maximillian Von Enger after himself, his name being Maximillian Wilhelm Von Enger, but Michelle wanted Billy to be Canadian, so she registered him as William. There weren't too many times where Michelle could win in a difference of opinion, but Max thought it too much of a bother to change Billy's birth certificate, and because he had taken the Von from his name before he married, he let the boy be called William. "Make sure you call him William," he had demanded, and for a while she did. However, when Billy reached school age, his friends, and then his family, called him Billy. So, William Maximillian Enger was called Billy by everyone but his father, who most of the time didn't call him anything.

Michelle didn't mind the names Max had picked out for their two daughters, Sonja and Anna. Though both had a European touch and were names of Max's relatives, the names suited them. Even if Michelle wanted her children to be truly Canadian, their German background and heritage could not be ignored. And, Michelle conceded, that heritage was one to be proud of so she encouraged their study and use of it. This tended to appease Max and he was far less aggressive with the girls than he was with Billy and herself. It was mostly on Michelle and Billy that he took out his anger and frustration. Billy didn't need any encouragement to leave home at the age of seventeen. He clashed with his father constantly and was the object of Max's temper many times.

Tears threatened as Michelle thought of her two daughters now both enrolled in the University. Just last week she had finished moving Anna in with her sister who had an apartment just a short distance from the campus. Anna, her baby, her little waif... Though her straight hair was nearly black, and her grey-green eyes hid under long curly dark lashes like her father's, Anna loved to be a quiet participant rather than a leader. Sitting on the bed as her daughters put their clothes into the closet, they laughed. "You'll have a good time in Europe," they told Michelle. "Just try not to get Daddy too upset. He wants to take you places he enjoyed as a child." Michelle tried to think how the trip would be, but nothing in her imagination could really tell her.

"I'll try," she told them. "It's just that I don't like being away from you for a whole month."

"But we're in classes, Silly," Sonja stated, her dark auburn curls tight against her head, her brown eyes large and bright. "We won't be home anyway, so you might as well try to enjoy this time. You deserve it."

Michelle remembered thinking, "Do I really deserve it?"

Her daughters were not aware of all the things that went on between her and Max. Billy knew but Michelle didn't know if the girls did.

"I know it will be a change," Anna had said in a voice that was suddenly older and more mature. "Daddy can be a little gruff with you, but think of this as a great adventure and that you're off experiencing something you've never done before. It'll be great!" she said with an exuberant bounce onto the bed. "You just have fun."

"I can't figure out where the time went." Michelle hugged Anna. "All of a sudden my family is grown and gone—even my baby," she laughed, holding her youngest away from her. "Come on, girls," shall we go to lunch before I have to get back home to my packing?"

Now as Michelle sat in the plane, Max sleeping soundly next to her and her favorite tune continuing her reflective mood, she thought again about her two girls. They were different in many ways. Sonja, now twenty, was strong and outgoing, with an unabrasive confidence, unlike that of her father's. She loved new experiences and new challenges. This led her to the study of languages at the university.

Anna was eighteen and a lot like Michelle, always tender and concerned about the welfare of others, maybe too much so. Many times she put aside her own wishes to help others. Her kindness was even evident in the number of bandaides she would place on her favorite teddy bear when he would fall off the bed. It was no surprise to anyone when Anna enrolled in the nursing program at the university. "I really want to go, Mama, and I would like to spend at least the first year with Sonja." Sonja was pleased to be able to take Anna under her wing, and that relieved Michelle of most of her anxieties at having her baby gone.

As people began opening their blinds, Michelle could see

that the darkness was gone. She sensed Max's hostility even before he spoke. "If I see you wearing those earphones in public again," he said with a snarl, "I'll smash them. Now go freshen up. We land in an hour."

Michelle opened her window shade before moving. The sky was clear and the ocean below lay like a cold blue blanket. A surge of adrenaline swept over her. This was almost like a dream. What beauty! If only things were different between her and Max, she might be excited, but her fears of him always took away anything that was pleasant. She stumbled over him to get out to the aisle. It felt good to stretch her legs as she made her way to the bathroom to tidy up. The sunshine gleamed in from every open blind and Michelle could feel its warmth. Maybe Sonja is right, she thought. This could be a new adventure.

Max didn't move or acknowledge her when she returned to her seat. He was too deeply engrossed in his book. Michelle had to give him a nudge to get by. With a snort he looked at her. "You look presentable enough to be my wife now," he said. "People will take notice."

For a second Michelle wanted to vomit. Who did he think he was? He had grown more and more demanding and arrogant over the years. When they were first married she thought he might change, but even after doting on him for twenty-four years nothing was different. In fact, his temper and aggression were worse. If there were problems at the office or even with an associate, he vented his anger at home—sometimes verbally, but more and more it was becoming physical, and she still had bruises to prove it. However, Michelle was not giving up. For some reason, she thought, if she persisted maybe she and Max could have a good marriage. And then there were the children. They were a family. She hoped that with Max visiting all his childhood haunts on this holiday he would mellow. That was the only reason she let herself be talked into taking this trip. Michelle had some misgivings but just maybe there was hope. Now, as she sat beside him on the plane the doubts were fast creeping in, but she knew she had a whole month. So, no matter what her fears were she would try to make this a good holiday. She realized though, that if she was going to cope at all some of her needs had to be met, especially if they didn't infringe on his. Turning to Max she said, "I am going to try to enjoy this trip with you. I will let you take me to all your childhood places but..." She said this with a tense slow emphasis, "sometimes when we are traveling and you're reading, I would like to listen to my music." There it was, said and irrevocable. What could he say or do in this crowd of people? Michelle felt a brief moment of safety.

Max was silent for a moment, a look of bewilderment lasting only a second. "You will not embarrass me, do you hear?" he commanded.

"No, I would never think of doing that," she retorted. Max was too shocked to react. The tone of her voice, a surprise even to Michelle, was something he had not heard before.

Everyone seemed to be busy now tidying up blankets, pillows, magazines and papers. The stewardesses were scurrying up and down the aisles. With a ding of a bell the captain's voice came over the loudspeaker. "Thank you for flying AirCanada Flight 831 to Paris and points beyond. We will be landing in approximately thirty minutes. Please take note of the seatbelt sign and remain seated until the plane has come to a complete stop and the signs have been shut off." As his voice repeated the message in fluent French, Michelle kept her gaze on the land masses and bodies of water below. The world was beautiful. The array of greens, browns, and blues that at first had blended soon began taking the form of towns and cities as the plane dropped lower. Cars were no longer just black dots on a ribbon of black. Trains snaked through treed countryside.

The plane bounced lightly on the tarmac and soon Max and Michelle were being pushed ahead by the throngs of people exiting the plane. They followed the main flow of traffic to the luggage chutes and waited. Michelle looked around at the foreign language on the signs and listened curiously to the scuttle of voices around her. Occasionally she could understand the odd word spoken. Maybe she could finally learn more of her high school French. That could be exciting she told herself.

It took over an hour to collect their baggage and get through customs. "I'll call a taxi," Max told her, and in his fluent French, and in a loud voice, he waved down a passing cab. He looked around to make sure those around him had heard his proficient use of the language. With an oversized grin he ushered Michelle into the back seat and waited for the driver to load their luggage. Michelle was glad to be in the car and away from all the people who had been looking at them. Who's embarrassed now? she asked herself.

"Hotel D'Azure," Max informed the driver, not caring if he spoke English or French. He didn't have to make an impression now.

Soon the taxi was racing down the highway and into the main part of Paris. People jammed the sidewalks, six and seven abreast. Traffic was four lanes deep coming and going. "Look at the shops, Michelle. You'll have fun shopping." Max's excitement was mounting. When the taxi turned north Michelle gasped. The street was wide, congested with cars and people. Stores and shops were on the right; regal looking hotels and parks were on the left. Straight ahead stood a giant archway and gate.

"The Arc D'Triumph," Max volunteered. "Isn't it magnificent? You are traveling down one of the most famous streets in Paris, the Champs D'Elysees." Max was so bubbly he couldn't sit back on his seat. He sat forward, head moving from side to side, so as to not miss anything. Michelle could feel an unexpected excitement at the new experience.

"If only..." she said unconsciously.

"If only what?" Max sat back beside her. Michelle had not realized her words were said outloud. "You're not going to wish the kids were here?"

"No," Michelle said quietly, but her heart said differently.

The taxi slowed and pushed its way through vehicles and pedestrians as it turned down a narrow roadway. Just as it reached a crowded intersection they tried to move through a green light. "Traffic lights don't mean a thing here," Max stated when he saw Michelle gasp at the protesting gestures of their driver.

The car stopped under some marble looking arches and Max got out. "Only the best," he said, pulling Michelle after him. He made some comment to the driver as he paid him and both men laughed aloud. Max was looking eagerly at Michelle but the driver was more discreet giving her only an awkward glance. Max strutted into the hotel, a wide grin spread across his face. Michelle followed like an obedient puppy.

"I wish you would straighten up and smile," Max told her on their way to the elevator.

"I'd like to," Michelle said trying to put some kindness into her voice, "if you'd remember I'm a person, too."

"What do you mean?" Max unlocked the door to their room.

"Making crude remarks at my expense. And," she added, "in a language I don't understand." She tossed her purse on the wine colored bedspread.

"You're just sensitive. Loosen up a bit. It was only a joke." Max disappeared into the bathroom and returned shortly twisting the corner of his oversized mustache. "Let's go walk the avenue and do some sightseeing for a bit. I don't want to waste any time." Jet lag made Michelle's already weary body protest but anything was better than staying here alone. Max would want to go to bed soon enough.

The smell that met them as they stepped out onto the street reminded Michelle of a midway carnival. She allowed Max to propel her through the crowd, across the street and onto the less crowded side of the Elysees. "What is the Champs D'Elysees, Max? What does it mean?" Michelle's query was genuine and Max beamed as he answered. "Champs means field and Elysees means Elysium so putting it together means Elysium Fields or translated Paradise or place of supreme delight."

"It is pretty isn't it? The lawns, the park-like appearance with the Arc on one end and the regal buildings on the other. I find it quite impressive." They stopped to watch a monkey beg for coins for a street vendor.

"Don't!" Max warned, but it was too late. Michelle had already dropped a coin into the little tin cup. "They're usually a scam, Michelle. You shouldn't cater to them."

"It was only a loonie."

"Canadian money!"

"Well, do I have anything else?" She looked hard at him.

"I guess I should give you some pocket money. You'll need some when you use the public bathrooms."

"You pay for the use of the bathroom?" They were walking again.

"Yes, they have attendants in all public toilets. It's all prim and proper."

"Like at the airport?"

Max nodded. "Whatever you do, don't call it a bathroom. It's a toilet. A bathroom is just that, rooms for bathing."

Michelle didn't comment. They walked until they came to

a parking lot. Michelle slumped down onto the bench. "I've had it," she said mostly to herself. The seagulls screeched overhead as they retrieved tossed-away scraps.

"Let's head back," Max said matter-of-factly. "We'll have an early supper and then go to bed. By tomorrow you'll have adjusted to the time change." The walk back was quicker. They only stopped once to look at some exotic modern fashions in a display window.

Once in the room Michelle kicked off her shoes and lay back onto the satiny cover of the bed. Instantly Max was beside her. "I can't wait to go to bed." His eyes were on her face while he caressed her upper arm.

Michelle tensed and abruptly sat up. "Let's eat first, "she said, trying to give her voice some zest she did not feel.

Slowly Max got up and without comment went to the phone where he ordered a meal to be brought up to their room. "I'm going to shower," he said, unbuttoning his shirt.

Michelle breathed a sigh of relief and again lay back on the bed. She took the walkman from the bag near her and turned it on. She was so tired she hurt. Even through the music she could hear Max moving around in the bathroom and wondered how she was ever going to change her feelings toward him. The soothing music reminded her of Anna. Even having the children had not closed the widening gap between herself and her husband, but Michelle was grateful for the experiences she had had with them. Max hadn't taken much interest in the children. He always seemed too busy or preoccupied. Maybe it was her fault he never took an interest. She took care of them when they were sick, and she tried to take them with her whenever she went out. Max didn't ever volunteer to take care of them or to be with them so Michelle just did it herself. When Max was home he grew impatient and intolerant with their childhood games and chitter-chatter. He criticized their mistakes and sibling rivalry, however slight. If they didn't get the best grades, or obtain the highest scores he would belittle them and call them dumb or stupid. He was so dictatorial that Michelle would protect her children by hiding anything that might encourage Max's reactions and anger toward them. It always seemed she was playing a game of survival for herself and her children.

A knock at the door made Michelle spring to her feet. Dizzy momentarily, she stopped to get her balance before opening the door. Max was right behind her in his dressing gown. Taking his wallet from the bureau he tipped the waiter and locked the door when he left.

"I expected you to be out of your traveling clothes," he said impatiently eyeing the earphones on the bed. "Now we're ready to eat."

"I was going to shower too, before I ate, but I'll wait," she told him as she quickly put away the walkman.

Max uncovered the food and pushed the trolley to the table near the window. "It smells good," Michelle said.

"It is good," Max informed her. "I ordered the best." He motioned to the chair across the table. Michelle took a seat as he opened the bottle of red wine. "I told you I was going to take advantage of everything on this trip. Nothing will be too good. And," he paused to pour some wine into her glass," that means European wine at all our meals." Michelle shivered at Max's enunciation of the word "everything" and watched him fill his stemmed glass.

The seafood platter tasted good and Michelle, sipping her wine, began to feel a little better. They watched the couples walking the avenue outside. It was all so foreign to her. "There's a lot of history here, isn't there?" she asked casually. "Everything can be dated back hundreds of years."

"Even thousands," Max added, his voice a bit softer.

"Tomorrow we'll do the town, from the Eiffel Tower to the museums and some parks—the works. Thursday you can shop in the morning and then we'll catch the train to the south of France. Eat up now so we can go to bed. It is early in the day but if we have a good sleep and get up in the morning, the effects of jetlag will be gone."

After eating, Max wheeled the cart out into the hallway and locked the deadbolt when he closed the door. "No need to be interrupted," he said glaring lustfully at his wife. "I intend to make love to you in every country we stop in," he told her as he unzipped her blouse.

"I-I was going to take a shower," Michelle said clutching her loose blouse close to her.

"After. I'm too tired to wait for you." He grabbed the blouse and threw it on the bed. "Your body is as sleek today as the day we were married. You are my little Barbie Doll." Max placed a wet kiss on her neck.

Michelle relented as always and Max pulled her to the bed. As usual there was little foreplay or intimacy in their love-making. Habit took over and automatically Michelle escaped into a world of her own. In her mind she ran through the hills where flowers danced in the breeze and the air was fresh from pine forests on the nearby mountains. She could see eagles soaring freely in the wind and she flew with them over the rainbow and into the clouds mindless to the grasping hands and rough kisses. All her actions were done by rote. She knew what satisfied him and, she permitted it. Max took the look of serenity on her face as her satisfaction. He turned away from her and promptly went to sleep. It was dark when Michelle came back to reality. Max's snoring, as was customary, confirmed that he was sleeping. Michelle slipped out of bed and into the shower where she scrubbed herself thoroughly.

Chapter Two

Max was as good as his word. He took Michelle to fine restaurants and clothing shops encouraging her to buy fashionable and trendy clothes. "Perfect clothes for a perfect body," he insisted. "You will be the envy of all Toronto in these French fashions." Every time Michelle mentioned money and the exorbitant costs, Max would brag, so that everyone could hear that nothing was too expensive for his wife. He waved his credit card around like the national flag. Michelle panicked at the thought of returning home with such an enormous credit card bill and no more savings. She knew how he hated her spending any of his money; she had to account for every dime. However, when he got the notion to spend it, it went through his fingers like scalding water. He waved off her protests to his spending telling her not to worry about it. This trip was worth it.

After she had agreed to buy two nice dresses with matching shoes, she refused to try on any more. He might have gotten over jet lag, but the walking, shopping, and trying on clothes exhausted her.

Later that day, Michelle waited at the train station while Max bought a train schedule. "It's a book!" Michelle exclaimed when he returned.

"It's the only thing to have." Max flopped onto the bench next to Michelle. "Look, it has every schedule for every train in

Europe. We got it made. We can plan our schedule to the very minute."

Michelle grimaced at Max's pleasure. Typical, she thought, everything has to be regimented. Stuffing the book into his money pouch, Max jumped up. "The TGV leaves for Lyon in fifteen minutes. Let's go!" He hurried her through hordes of people and luggage, dragging their suitcases with them. Shortly they were on the farthest loading platform where only a handful of people waited. Michelle stopped to catch her breath. Before them stood a bright orange streamlined giant.

"It looks like a bullet," Michelle said, touching the smooth sleek surface of the engine.

"That's exactly what it is. The fastest moving train on European rails."

"What does TGV stand for?" Michelle asked as Max passed their tickets to the conductor.

"The literal translation means the train of the fastest speed. My book says it established a world record in 1981 of 380 kilometers an hour. Normally on this line from Paris to Lyon it goes about 260 kilometers an hour."

The TGV shot down the track so fast Michelle could hardly see the countryside. Max was so engrossed in the schedule book he paid little attention to his surroundings or to Michelle. For once she listened to her music undisturbed by Max's objections. She was glad when they changed trains in Lyon so she could enjoy the scenery. Once on the slower train Michelle marvelled at the contrast between the horse and mule drawn carts in the vineyards and huge modern factories and nuclear power plants. Modernization was okay but Michelle liked the relaxing atmosphere of the country farms and fields of grazing sheep.

"I think we'll get off in Toulon and do some shopping." Michelle was watching the Rhône River go by as Max spoke. "I want to get some local maps to find two of the cities where we used to go for holidays when I was a kid." He thumbed through more pages. "Here they are. Sanary and the harbor town of Port Issol. Michelle glanced at him with a little smile, but went back to looking at the moving scenery.

"Excuse me, Sir." An English gentleman came around to talk to Max. "I picked up one of those train schedules in Paris and can't figure out how to use it. The chap at the kiosk said it would keep my wife," he motioned to the lady across the aisle, "and I on schedule this whole holiday."

Max straightened taller in his seat, his chest swelling. "Anyone can follow this book."

The gentleman hesitated at Max's haughtiness but cautiously asked, "Could you show me?"

Michelle leaned forward and smiled kindly at the elderly lady who was watching her husband talk to Max. Not waiting to be invited, she stepped around the two men who were now engrossed in the train book and introduced herself.

"Hello, I'm Michelle Enger," she said.

"Hello," came the pleasant reply. "I hope George wasn't too forward asking for help. He sure struggled with that book."

"No," Michelle assured her. "Max just sounds a little strong sometimes."

"My name is Betty Harrison. Are you going to Toulon?"

"To start with. My husband spent some time there when he was growing up."

"Is he French?"

"No, his family is from Germany, but he had been all over Europe as a boy. We live in Canada now."

"George and I are from Bristol, England. George served in France during the war so he decided to bring me over for a visit before we get too much older."

"Thank you for your help," Michelle heard George say.

"Anytime," Max replied, his head held high as George approached the two women.

"Thank you for your visit, Michelle. Maybe we'll meet again."

"That would be nice," Michelle said as she stepped back over Max.

"Can't imagine anyone not being able to figure out that book," Max spouted. "It's so easy."

"I think you astonished Mr. Harrison," Michelle whispered aloud once she was beside him. "I wish you wouldn't come across so strongly to other people."

Max glared at her. "You're exaggerating," he snapped. "It's just my resonant voice."

"I think you enjoy intimidating people, Max." Michelle stopped, surprised at herself for speaking out. Biting her bottom lip she slumped back into her chair.

Max hissed, his face inches from hers. "Some people need to be intimidated. It keeps them in their place."

Michelle sat stiffly her eyes on her folded hands. She was glad when the train slowed and finally rolled to a stop. She followed Max out of the car.

"Smell the change in the air," Max said as they walked out of the station after storing their luggage—his anger forgotten by the nostalgia he felt. The air did seem heavier to Michelle but not oppressive. Palm trees lined the sidewalks and floral arrangements decorated everything including the median in the middle of the wide streets. There were lots of people about but there was no congestion like there had been in Paris and the pace was much slower.

"This is what I want you to buy, Michelle." Max pointed to an assortment of swim wear in a shop window.

"What on earth for? I don't swim."

"You're not coming all the way to the south of France and not take a dip in the Mediterranean," he demanded and entered the store.

"I'm forty-two years old, Max. I can't wear those things."

Max turned sharply. "Look around you, Woman. You're not in colonial Canada now, so get with it."

The tingling of a bell announced the arrival of another customer. Both Max and Michelle moved to let him by but Michelle couldn't help smiling at Max's disgusted snort. Strapped to the customer's grey hair was a set of earphones with music so loud they could hear it. Michelle's spirits suddenly rose and she couldn't help but feel a sense of triumph. This man was much older than she was.

The matter of the swim suits still remained unsettled so she busied herself trying to find one she might consider wearing. She swallowed hard every time she shook her head at the flimsy two-piece bikinis that Max showed her. Finally a clerk rescued her, "Madam? I have others in the back that may be more to your liking. Come..."

Michelle followed the woman into a back room where more cupboards lined the walls. "These will be for you. Sort through them and try on any you like. The dressing room is free."

"Thank you," Michelle said and picked up a solid black one-piece suit. It was modest yet streamlined; she instantly liked it. She hoped Max would as well. It did accentuate her still shapely figure. "I found one," she told him.

Max looked at it, no facial expression to relieve Michelle's mind, but after paying for it and walking across to a little outdoor restaurant, he said, "You can model that for me when we get to Bandol. That's where I've decided to stay tonight. It may not be a bikini but it looks like it will show off enough of your body." He paused as he leaned closer. "I like to show off

21

what's mine." Michelle shuddered, hoping Max didn't notice.

The train trip to Bandol was a memorable experience. Michelle was glad Max found the sunset appealing and striking enough to photograph. The brilliant orange reflected on the clear glass water of the Mediterranean. The sun turned a majestic cerise as it slid behind the dark shoreline which was silhouetted against the sky. By the time the train stopped and the sea was out of sight, the sky was shades of blue, grey and mauve. Michelle filed the memory of this celestial sunset into her mind for future fantasies.

"Hotel D'Oasis," Max ordered the taxi driver when they left the train. The hotel was alive with activity when they arrived, even though it seemed to be in a remote part of town. The porter took the Engers' luggage to the second floor. Michelle was exhausted. Whether it was from the final stages of jet lag or the stress of the day, the bed looked appealing.

"Good idea," Max stated as if reading her thoughts. "But first we'll have a swimsuit fashion show, then we'll have some fun." He held up a small bag he'd drawn from his pocket. "I bought a new suit as well." Michelle felt like smacking the cheshire grin spread on his face, but that would have placed her in the same abusive category as he was in.

Throwing her purse onto the bed, she headed for the bathroom to change. She did not want to undress in front of Max. He didn't need any encouragement by seeing her put the swimsuit on. She also hoped that if she took her time Max would fall asleep, but even though her every move was deliberate she could hear Max moving around. Finally she just decided to get it over with before Max got angry. He turned as she exited the bathroom. He stood naked except for a skimpy bikini suit. "Super piece of manhood you married, eh?" He ran his hands down the sides of his body. "Come here, Woman!" Nausea sent a wave of perspiration over Michelle.

Someday, Michelle Clarkson Enger, this guy's not going to order you around, she thought, as she let Max pull her toward him. The majestic sunset she had filed away in her memory, once again pulled her into her fantasy world. Finished, he turned away. They both slept.

In the morning Max was the first to move. He stretched his naked body, threw off the covers, and slid out of bed. Peering through the shutters he said, "It's overcast today so maybe we should go to Grasse and save the beach until it's sunnier." He grabbed his robe off the chair. "I'll shower first, and then while you're showering I'll make up our day's itinerary. I'll show it to you at breakfast," he added as he shut the bathroom door.

"All right," Michelle yawned and pulled the covers back over her.

"Up, Woman!" Max grabbed the sheet and pulled it off her. "Or I'll make love to you right now! You're so delectable!"

Michelle was on her feet in one move. "Just joking," Max laughed and Michelle escaped into the bathroom.

It was an hour's bus ride to Grasse on the French Riviera. Michelle could smell a strong bittersweet aroma as soon as they stepped off the bus. Acres of flowers covered the hillsides and open areas in the city. "I wanted this to be a surprise," Max said. "What do I buy you every birthday or anniversary?"

"Perfumes and colognes," Michelle replied, smelling the inside of her wrist where she had applied some this morning.

"Well, now you can see the real thing. Frogengard Perfume Factory is world famous. Here every exotic scent is manufactured; Chanel is the most well-known."

They paid the admission to the factory and spent the next two hours watching craftsmen experiment with scents, walking among the storage and aging vats, and smelling sample after sample until Michelle could hardly distinguish one perfume from another. Max's arms were full of bottles and containers of perfumes, sachet, and colognes. "You wish to purchase all of these, Monsieur?" the clerk asked.

"I won't have to buy any more for a life time," he answered loudly and dropped the load onto the counter.

Michelle reddened and walked away. She could hear Max speaking noisily to another couple while his purchases were being totalled. He stopped short at the sound of the price, then sheepishly tossed his credit card on the counter. "Easy come, easy go," he said with a short laugh. "These are the most popular in the world." He patted the bag he was holding.

It was a relief to be outside in the fresh air after the intoxicating heaviness in the factory. Max and Michelle wandered the streets looking at the shops, the art on the building walls, and the beautiful gardens. Every block seemed to have a perfume factory of one size or another. Fruit and vegetable stands lined the streets under over-sized canopies.

Michelle never mentioned the perfume until they returned to the hotel in Bandol. Max carelessly dropped the contents of the bag on the table. "Don't break any," Michelle cautioned. She took the tie out of her long hair and flipped it loose as she spoke.

"You haven't looked at them or even said thank you," Max snarled.

Michelle was tired and worn out and too weak to resist her pent-up feelings. She spun around. "I don't ever say anything to you on how you spend the money," she challenged, "and as much as I know perfume is your thing, this," and she motioned with her arm, "is ridiculous. I won't use all this in two lifetimes!"

Max jumped to his feet, meeting her challenge. "These are the elite, Woman, and you'll never get them so cheap anywhere else."

Fear suddenly enveloped her. "I do appreciate the thought

but I-I think it was a bit much."

Max backed away his tone calmer. "You'd better be grateful, Woman."

As Michelle brushed her teeth she could hear Max mumbling angrily in the bedroom. "What is it?" she asked when she saw him searching the room when she came out.

"Where did you put my wallet?" he asked without facing her. Clothes were strewn all over the bed from the suitcases. His black hair was askew, his shirt tail hung from his pants.

"Pardon me?" Michelle exclaimed.

"Where did you put my wallet?" he glowered at her. Michelle backed away. His face was white with rage.

"Me? Since when have you ever allowed me to have money. You haven't even given me any toilet change."

Max ignored her comment as he went back to rummaging through their luggage. Michelle followed after him, searching and folding as she replaced the clothes. "Where did you have it last?" she asked timidly. "Maybe we can trace it back from there."

"I had it at Frogengard." He straightened, a new thought coming to mind. "I know, I was pick pocketed. I bet some street tramp took it right out of my pocket." His voice rose and he marched over to the open window as if to see someone running away with his wallet.

"Let's not accuse anyone, Max, until we search thoroughly. You could have dropped it someplace too."

He spun to face her. "I'm no kid, you know."

"I know that," Michelle replied meekly, "but I'll keep looking here if you want to retrace your steps back to the lobby. Maybe it was turned in."

"Now you have better eyes than me, eh?" he demanded.

"No, just..."

"Oh, never mind," and he slammed the door as he left

the room.

It took Michelle a few minutes to sort things but when she went to pick up the empty perfume bag she spotted something on the floor under the corner of the bed. She picked up the wallet, pushed back some of the Canadian dollars that had escaped, and set it on the dresser. While she waited for Max's return she sat in front of the mirror to brush out her hair. There was no admiration in her reflection; it was just something to do.

"That was a lost cause!" Max hollered as he came back into the room. "Made me feel like a jer-er...!"

Michelle pointed to the bureau then turned her attention back to the mirror. She could see Max counting the money in his wallet. Turning around to face him, her heart pounding, she said, "Can I ask a question?"

"Humph." Max responded without looking up.

"Why are you carrying so much Canadian cash? You planned on using the credit card while on this holiday."

"I always carry cash, remember?" The sneer in his voice showed in the dagger-look of his eyes. "It's good for my image."

"But there's so much..."

He snapped before she could finish. "What did you do? Snoop?"

"I picked the wallet off the floor. Some of the money had slipped out."

Michelle sat down on the bed directly in front of him. Ignoring his rudeness she gathered her courage. "Do you have to carry it all in one place? We were lucky this time." She stopped to give him time to respond. When he didn't speak, she added sarcastically, "I don't want misfortune to spoil anything for you."

Max remained silent so Michelle placed her hairbrush

on the dresser and climbed into bed. She picked up a hotel magazine to read while she waited. Sometime later Max came to bed. Michelle quickly switched off her light. Breathlessly she waited for movement from the other side of the bed, but soon she could hear Max's heavy breathing. Relieved, she turned away and drifted into a relaxing sleep.

The sun streaming onto Michelle's face from a crack in the window shutter woke her the next morning. Max was seated on one of the easy chairs counting his money and placing it into piles on the table.

"I want you to hide half this money in one of your suit-cases." He spoke without a greeting. "I can't afford to have it all disappear if it gets lost again."

Michelle crossed the room and waited for Max to hand her a stack of bills. "Count them," he told her. When he began counting his pile, she sat down to count hers. "Twenty," she said giving them to him.

"Good." He fanned the hundred dollar bills, then handed them back to her. "I want you to put these in a safe place. I'll ask for them when I need to change some into francs or lire." With that command he grabbed his robe and went into the bathroom.

Within seconds the water was running.

Michelle sat spellbound in disbelief. In her hand she held twenty one hundred dollar bills. For a moment she felt panicky but a faint hope glimmered in her heart. Was he changing? Will this holiday be a good thing for their marriage after all? And he didn't get too angry when she asked him about the money. Maybe there was hope. Michelle went to her suitcase where she carefully placed the money in her little compact sewing kit.

Later, when she came from the bathroom to dress, Max was seated in his robe reading the travel book. "Put your swim suit on now. It's going to be a nice warm day so we can go to the beach."

"Can't I change when I get there?' she questioned as she tied her hair back. "I don't like walking around in my swimsuit."

"Look around you. Half the population is in swim suits." Max strutted over to her tossing his robe onto the bed. He was already dressed in his new suit. "I'm going as I am," he told her.

"I'll just wear my clothes over it," she conceded.

Once they were dressed, Max handed Michelle some French francs. "Toilet money," he said simply.

After a continental breakfast in their room, Max and Michelle took the bus to Port Issol. Stretching in front of them as they strolled down the palm laden streets was the Mediterranean Sea in all its cerulean splendor. Michelle didn't say anything but she was pleased Max had chosen to put some clothes over his brief swim wear.

Numerous people were already on the beach, but only a few were in the water. Max immediately stripped down and dove off the rocky edge. Michelle could hear him gasp as he hit the water. As fast as he went in, Max was out again.

Michelle knew enough not to comment. She continued to step out of her slacks while she watched her husband lay on the warm sand. She walked over and touched the water with her toe. No wonder he was out like a flash, she chuckled to herself as she swooshed her foot back and forth. This water was cold.

Michelle could see coral-type rocks and small fish in the deeper water. She walked slowly down the sandy edge, both feet in the cold but refreshing sea. As soon as her feet grew accustomed to the temperature, Michelle walked further into the water. It didn't take her long to get her whole body submerged and she lay on her back to float aimlessly.

"You're nuts," she heard Max exclaim sometime later.

She stood in the water, swirling her arms around in the coolness.

"It's lovely once you get used to it." Her eyes danced, bringing a youthful glow to her face. The cold water made her body tingle and she felt alive and vibrant. Michelle, enjoying this new experience, was oblivious to the effect her childish innocence was having on Max. He watched her shiver then immerse herself back into the water. "It's too cold to stay out," she called and awkwardly swam away.

Max took a step into the water and stopped. The coldness hit him like ice. "Come out of there!" he called before she had gone too far. Michelle stood, questioning the unknown expression on his face. "Come out of there right now. It'll make you sick. It's far too cold for any sane human."

A sudden sweep of fear engulfed Michelle almost making her sick. Max's tone was always harsh and severe but something was different somehow. The look on his face and in his dark brown eyes reminded her of something evil. She slowly made her way out of the water not taking her eyes off him. As she approached him, her skin red and tingly from the cold, she watched Max's expression change from anger to lust. She watched him as he ran his gaze greedily up and down her body. Her heart began to beat rapidly. Max grabbed her and pulled her to him. She could feel his body stiffen as he roughly placed his mouth on hers, his hands moving rapidly up and down her back. "You're beautiful," he gasped, hardly able to breath. "I want to make love to you right here on the beach." His hands slowed to caress Michelle's cool skin. She pulled away as soon as his grasp loosened. "You're mine, Woman," Max panted.

Michelle could see other tourists watching them. She spun on her heel. "I'm not about to forget it either." She surprised herself as she continued, "But I draw the line at some things." She picked up her clothes and walked toward a change room.

Max ran up beside her and snarled, "You're embarrassing me."

Michelle glanced around her at the other tourists. "I'm sorry," she said sincerely, "but I do have some self-respect. You're not taking that from me."

"What did you think I was going to do? Make love on the beach?"

"Isn't that what you had in mind?" Michelle asked flatly.

"What do you think I am?" he shrilled, " An animal?"

"Yes," Michelle replied matter-of-factly.

The back of Max's hand caught her across the mouth and she staggered. Hatred welled up inside her and tears streamed down her face. She pulled open the changing room door and went inside. As she wiped away the trickle of blood from her lips, she could hear Max grumbling outside. She sat on the built-in bench, her head in her hands, and sobbed. "What came over me?' she asked herself in a whisper. "Why did I say what I did? It's not like me." Leaning her head against the moist wall she closed her eyes and tried to think of her next move. Max was now so angry she didn't know what he was capable of. "What am I going to do?" she cried softly.

"I'm ready to go," she heard Max call.

She changed quickly, her mind trying to think of her different options. Her first thought was to escape, but not knowing how, she erased that thought fast. I might as well face him and get it over with, she told herself. All he could do was hit her again as he often did. She would apologize and hope that would aid her cause. Somehow she doubted it.

Cautiously she stepped out onto the sand. "I'm sorry, Max," she apologized. "I guess I wasn't thinking."

"You should be." He stalked up to her. "I don't ever want you to behave like that again." He clasped her hand tightly in his. "That's twice since we started this trip you've tried to usurp my authority."

"I'm sorry," repeated Michelle. "I'll try not to anger you again." She could feel the eyes of the world on them and she warmed with embarrassment, her knees almost too weak to walk.

"We're going back to Bandol," Max told her, "You're shivering. I knew that water was too cold." Michelle didn't argue. The southern sun was warming so she knew it was not from the cold water.

They walked silently to the bus station, had a coffee and caught the bus back to Bandol. Michelle gazed at the scenery going by but her thoughts were back at the beach. She remembered her feeling of freedom and vibrancy as she swam in the sea. She was a poor swimmer but that didn't mar the exhilaration she felt. She recalled the disturbing emotion she had seen on Max's face and the dagger in his eyes as he watched her from the water's edge. The fear crept over her again for a moment then somewhere in the back of her mind something flashed. Max had been out of control and when she thought about it, she almost felt a sense of power. A new sense of power over Max? How can I have power over him? He won the battle back there like he always does. Michelle glanced at her husband, who again was reading his travel book, while he twitched the corner of his straggly mustache. Still, the more she thought about it, the more she realized the truth of it. The thought was very disturbing.

Back at the hotel, Michelle decided to have a quick shower to wash off the sea water. As she stepped out, Max was waiting for her, the new swim suit she had purchased in his hands. "Put this on," he ordered.

"It's wet and cold."

Max snatched away her towel, and Michelle shuddered.

"Fine," he pulled her to the bed, "it will save me from ripping it off."

Michelle cried in protest, but Max was already too busy to hear. Escaping to the hills had always worked, especially when Max was abusive. But today, Michelle found escape impossible. The pain Max was inflicting kept her mind alert and conscious. She was still crying, huddled under the blankets, long after Max had dressed.

Michelle's body throbbed as she showered for a third time that day. She let the water run hot over her trying to loosen her aching muscles. Her body began to feel better but nothing could wash off the degradation she felt. Michelle scrubbed her body till it burned to try to rid herself of the urge to escape. She would do nothing to infuriate Max again, she promised herself, but subconsciously a discomforting thought began to glow. Pushing it into the back of her mind, she left the bathroom.

"What took so long," Max asked as she reapplied her makeup. "I'm starving."

"I won't be a minute," she responded as if nothing had happened.

"This is the dress I want you to wear tonight." Max held in his hand a brocade dress with brightly-colored flowers. Before Michelle could protest, Max continued, "With the hood, it gives you a mysterious air. Every man's eyes will be on my wife." He emphasized the word *wife* as he helped her on with the dress.

Michelle looked into the mirror. Even though she liked what she saw, she wanted to rip it off. Why does he make me feel so cheap? With a sigh she gave her loosely hanging hair a final flip and together they left the room.

Michelle was grateful for the heavy brocade that provided warmth in the cool fall air. Max was handsomely dressed in solid grey slacks, set off by a mid-weight yellow pullover. He carried his wool tweed jacket over his arm. Max's sleek, well proportioned body held no appeal for Michelle. She knew what lay beneath that smooth exterior. However, as they entered the restaurant she knew that they had turned many of the people's heads.

The discontent Michelle felt expressed itself in the stiff yet graceful moves of her body as she walked down the promenade to the night club after supper. Max seemed a little gentler with her as he guided her around the dance floor. They sat out to sip drinks during the more lively numbers. Those dances didn't hold any appeal for Max, she remembered. He liked the waltzes where he could spin her around the floor showing off in front of everyone.

Michelle was exhausted. If only bedtime could be the wonderful reprieve it was meant to be after a trying day. Max was riding high. All the way back to the hotel he had bragged about his dancing skills and how everybody had watched them. Once into bed, Michelle snuggled under the covers and turned away from Max when he crawled in next to her. He ran his hands down her body protesting, "Too bad I'm tired tonight." He nipped at the back of her neck, then settled back into his pillow.

Michelle said a silent prayer of thanks and slipped into a peaceful sleep.

Chapter Three

The rest of the week in the South of France remained relatively peaceful. Michelle allowed herself to be toured to every place of interest there was including vineyards and wineries. As long as she didn't say or do anything to upset her husband, the days went pleasantly by.

Max had worked out an itinerary for their trip to Italy, so with his enthusiasm for trains, they left their hotel in time to catch the 8:00 p.m. train to Pisa, then to Florence. "This'll be an adventure for you, another first," Max said bustling Michelle into the taxi. "We'll get a sleeper for the night."

People were milling about when Max and Michelle stepped out at the station. Michelle looked around apprehensively. "Sure lots of people trying to catch this train," she said, placing her suitcases on the cart Max had found abandoned nearby.

"Don't worry. We have our rail passes so we have first class preference. These people are peasants and ride the coach cars. Stay close." Pushing through the crowd Max elbowed himself and the cart up to an open door of the train. Michelle tried her best to keep up but as soon as Max split the crowd it closed up again, and it took all her strength to get to Max without being rude. When she finally reached him, Max was exchanging words with a French porter, the rail passes waving in his hand. The porter said something to Max that Michelle couldn't understand but Max's response left no doubt as to what was said. His face reddened, his eyes flared, and he began to yell. The porter kept pointing him toward the front of the train where people were lined up waiting to board.

"Max?" Michelle tried to get his attention. "Let's just move down." She picked her words carefully as she took hold of his arm.

Max pulled away, his virulent shouts carrying above the crowd. "Come on, Max," Michelle pleaded.

"I'm not leaving until we get a sleeper!" Max waved an angry fist at the porter who now had his back to Max trying to ignore him. "This jerk says these passes are only good for sleepers if we book in advance!"

"That sounds reasonable. Can you imagine what more bedlam this would be if they didn't book ahead?"

"What do you know about it?" Max's glare made her shiver. "Or don't you care if we have to pile in like animals?"

Michelle shook her head. Somewhere down the rail a train man called and clouds of steam shot onto the track.

"Shall we go back to the hotel?" Michelle asked, almost afraid to speak.

"This is a night train so there has to be somewhere to sleep." Max dragged the luggage nearer to the front of the train. Michelle followed through the thinning crowd. Another porter ushered them and their luggage into a car and before they could get their balance, the train jumped forward. Max stumbled. Swearing aloud he steadied himself and ordered the porter to find them a place to sleep. Without speaking the porter led them to a compartment and opened the door. Michelle heard him mention something about a 'couchette.' She looked in. Cramped into the tiny room were two sets of bunks, three tiers high. Max pushed past the small man and tossed his money

36

pouch on a lower bunk near the door. "Fine! We have to spend the next twelve hours sleeping like stacked sardines."

Two more couples jammed into the confined area before Michelle could claim a bunk. Max had already thrown his possessions onto the bottom bunk and the French passengers had claimed all but a top one. Michelle didn't hesitate. She put her carry-on bag and purse on the top bunk, then lifted the smaller suitcase. Her second case was heavier. She took a deep breath and lifted. Immediately the weight was taken from her. One of the men lifted it for her. "Thank you," Michelle said in English. He returned the gesture with a smile. Max stood in the aisle huffing and puffing waiting for some space to manoeuvre his bags. Michelle could hear him mumbling as she climbed to the top bunk and pushed her luggage to the foot of the bed. The space from the bed to the roof made it impossible to sit up but even with her suitcases at the foot she had room to lie down. With a sigh she put her head down, letting Max worry about himself.

The train moved slowly but noisily out of the station. The four other passengers in Michelle's couchette chatted freely in French. Max pushed himself between two women who were speaking across the aisle so he could get to Michelle "This is so stupid. What did we buy these special passes for if we end up like this?"

"It's all right for one night, isn't it?" Michelle tried to sound excited.

"You probably like it! You can sleep by yourself!"

"Max!" Michelle raised up, hitting her head on the ceiling.

"True, isn't it? " Max backed out of the couchette not caring who he bumped into. "I'm going to get some air." The women continued to babble, but their eyes and actions were focused in Max's direction.

Michelle lay back on the tiny pillow and closed her eyes. The clickety-clack of the train was soothing and she found herself humming a tune to the lulling rocking motion of the car. Yes, she told herself feeling only a little bit guilty. It is true. I can sleep by myself.

"American?" a broken accent asked.

Michelle turned to answer. "Canadian," she said to the youth who had lifted her suitcase.

"Aah, Montreal, Toronto, Calgary Stampede." He grinned and Michelle couldn't help but smile as his hazel eyes lit up his long angular face. "Tourist?" he asked. Michelle nodded, an unexpected yawn interrupting. "Bon Nuit," he added and stepped away.

Michelle turned to say good night, but stopped short when she saw Max standing in the doorway, his lips tight, his eyes narrow. She wanted to turn away but his glare riveted her to him. In two strides he was by her bunk. "You like them young?" he asked seductively.

Michelle was speechless. Max really did have a problem and it was getting worse. What made her think he might change? Max gave her face a squeeze. "Good night, Wife." His voice was a harsh order.

Michelle lay quiet for a moment to gather her strength. She rubbed the part of her face where she still felt the imprint of Max's fingers. She lay silent until she could hear him unzip his luggage to retrieve his science fiction book. The other passengers were also quiet. Were they afraid of Max's violent actions? Finally Michelle moved. After taking off her shoes she collected her walkman from her carry-on bag and was soon enjoying her private moment.

Michelle woke as the train clattered and jerked. It took her a second to orient herself to where she was. Her clothes felt heavy and her body ached as she turned, but she had slept well.

The bed opposite was empty, as was Max's. In fact, Michelle realized she was alone in the compartment. She jumped to the floor and tidied herself the best she could. Feeling a bit better she stood in the aisle of the train watching the scenery pass by while she waited for Max. The foggy dismal weather outside shrouded the drab and dirty buildings. Trash and garbage littered the ground and fences. This was Italy? It was sure different from what Michelle had expected. The train lurched to a stop. For an instant Michelle felt a sense of panic. She went to her bunk where she pulled her suitcases and carry bag down to the floor. She began to pull them out into the aisle. "Where are you going, Wife?"

For a moment Michelle thought she was going to cry. She didn't know if it was from disappointment or relief. She looked up at her husband who was dressed in wrinkle free, clean clothes, his suitcase in his hand. "Think I'd left you," he laughed as he pushed his way past her and into the couchette. "Now, that would have been interesting, wouldn't it?" Michelle was too hurt to respond. As she watched him she just wanted to wipe that smug look off his face.

"There's a bathroom down the hall. Once we leave the station you can clean up. You look a mess."

"W-We're not getting off here?"

He gave her a smirk, his voice mimicking hers. "No. This isn't Florence." He chuckled as he sat on the nearest bunk and opened up the travel book. Michelle stood rigid until her conscience eased her anger, then she grabbed her suitcase and went to change clothes. While she washed and dressed in the tiny bathroom, Michelle had to fight the anger that made her want to strike out at Max, to scream back at him. It was unusual for her to feel so strong about fighting back; maybe it was being away from home, in neutral territory. It did surprise her, however, and she almost wished the feeling would go away. Being passive was much easier. Whatever was happening it took all her strength, all her courage, to freshen up and return to her husband.

While waiting for a taxi at the station in Florence, Max went to one of the window bays to exchange his money into Italian lire. Michelle waited with the luggage as she watched people scurrying out of the building and into the bright sunshine. On their way to the Pension Zurigo, the taxi took them near the Signora Piazza, a town square lined with Greek statues of various sizes. The statue of David was one that Michelle recognized but was astonished to find it covered with pigeons and bird litter. Scaffolding leaned against many buildings and Michelle watched the crowds walking in and around them as if they were a regular part of the plaza. Some people were feeding the birds, others scurried in and out of shops. The taxi stopped in front of a grey building surrounded by a tall iron fence. Max pushed open the door, handed the driver some money, and after collecting their cases, herded Michelle into the Pension.

"This is an old city filled with history," Max told Michelle over lunch at their Pension. "I want you to take note of the masters when we visit some of the galleries. The culture will be good for you."

Michelle put on an artificial smile and let him expound his apparent knowledge of the artists. She would've been excited about the museums and galleries if she didn't have to listen to Max. If only there was something he knew nothing about. Michelle almost laughed aloud at that wish. There probably was, but she was too intimidated by him to find out. She sobered as he led her into the Uffizi Gallery with artists like Cenni di Pepo, Grotto di Bondone, Santa Cecilia, Masaccio and the world renowned DaVinci. The ceilings, walls, and even the floors were magnificent works of art, and a person could spend a lifetime there without seeing everything.

They strolled across the Pont de Vecchio, or Bridge of Gold Merchants. Here Max wanted her to buy some gold jewelry. "Some of these things will look great on you," he said pulling her up to a display case.

"Let's buy something for the kids," Michelle suggested. "I already have lots of new things to take home."

Max turned abruptly. "You don't buy gold for kids!"

"Our kids are adults, Max."

"You don't have to remind me. They've made me an old man." Max walked over to another case.

"You aren't old," Michelle said, hoping he'd take this as a compliment.

"I'm not old in the bedroom, am I?" He faced her squarely, a sickly grin from ear to ear. "I bet I'd surprise them at how good I am in that department."

Michelle glared at him, turned, and stomped out of the store. Max followed, grabbing her by the arm. Michelle was angry and didn't care what she said. "Sex and Money! Is that all you think about!" She pulled her arm away and fled. Max froze. His wife didn't speak to him like that. How dare she? Who did she think she was? He watched her turn the corner before he moved.

It was near dinner time and the sidewalk was full of shoppers and tourists. At first he couldn't see her, but then he caught a glimpse of her entering the Pitti Palace with a tour group just getting off a bus. He ran.

Michelle darted into the crowd of people. She had no idea where she was or where she was going. The rooms in the building she had entered were much the same as the art gallery she had been in earlier and she had no desire to look at more pictures. She stopped for a second to get her bearings, then noticed an open door that appeared to go outside. She didn't look behind; she just aimed for the open door ahead.

As she stepped outside she was taken back by the instant beauty of the garden. Green lush grass, beds or ornamental blossoms, delicately trimmed shrubs and trees, and a large fountain of spraying water. A full-sized statue of Neptune holding a poised spear stood in the center of the fountain. Forgetting Max and all those around her, she walked straight to the fountain. She was so emotionally and physically drained she just wanted to sit down and take in all this beauty. As she sat on the fountain's edge watching the goldfish in the water, an American voice spoke, "I hope he doesn't get one."

"Wh-What?" Michelle jumped up.

"I said, I hope he doesn't get one." Michelle looked up into a pleasant face, warm with a friendly smile.

"Oh, I hope he doesn't either. They're so beautiful."

"I think he's their protector and the spear is for the sharks lurking in the rocks."

"I hope you're right." She smiled slightly.

"A smile is much more appealing on such a perfect afternoon," he said placing his hands in his pants pockets. His light brown hair was a bit tousled; his polo shirt open at the neck gave him a casual air. "A beautiful smile, for a beautiful lady."

The compliment was so unexpected, Michelle blushed. But before she could comment... "Wife!" Max grabbed her before she could flee. "What are you trying to do?" he yelled at the American. "Pick up my wife!"

The stranger didn't fall to the challenge. "She's worth a common courtesy from a fellow American," the man replied calmly.

"We're not Capitalist Americans!" Max sneered as he yanked Michelle away. "We're Canadian!"

"You're beastly," Michelle said to Max, her anger returning. "How can you be so rude? He was just being friendly."

Max dragged Michelle up the sidewalk. "Let's get out of here before you get any more friendly notions. Maybe this holiday wasn't such a good idea." Max pulled Michelle back through the building, the vice-like grip making her hand numb.

Michelle was angry. "This holiday was your idea not mine," she challenged without thinking.

Max was near the boiling point by the time they reached the outside of the Palace. "I warned you about getting lippy." Michelle ducked as Max raised his arm and missed. A group of noisy students saved her from another try but Michelle knew she was in trouble. Max's arm dropped but he kept hold of his wife all the way back to the Pension. Michelle took these silent moments to chastise herself yet again. She couldn't understand why she'd become so vocal. She would never do this at home. As they entered the building, Michelle's fear turned to panic. Max was angry. I wish I had never spoken to that American, she said to herself.

It was getting dark by the time Max had pulled her to their room. Even when he unlocked the door he didn't release her hand. She was his prisoner. Trying to appease him quickly before he could hurt her, Michelle spoke, "I did it again, didn't I?" she grovelled. "I don't know what has come over me. Please forgive me." Max pushed her toward the bed and threw her down on it. His outstretched arm caught her off guard and the blow dropped her to her knees on the floor. Before she could rise, Max slapped a heavy hand across her head. "That's where you belong, wife. On your knees at the feet of your husband!"

"Max! Don't! You're hurting me!"

Max grabbed her by the hair pushing her head back to face him. "And so I should! You were completely out of hand today. For some reason you have been lippy and rebellious, just like a kid. You need to be reminded who's boss around here."

Michelle cowered closer to the bed as Max stripped off his clothes. The side of the bed stopped her from pulling away, and she couldn't escape because Max towered above her, his feet pressing her to the bed. The floor was hard under Max's weight and his rough hands caused her to squirm with discomfort. "Be still!" he hissed, as he pinned her arms above her head. "You asked for this." Michelle sucked in a deep breath, and once more let Max have his way.

The night was endless, but Michelle never left the cold floor even when her shaking body was finally released of its burden. Max lay sprawled on the bed above her, his breathing heavy. Michelle was far too ill to move. There wasn't a spot on her that didn't hurt. She knew there were bruises on her wrists where Max had held her, and one on the side of her face where he had knocked her down but she couldn't understand why the rest of her body hurt—why her whole lower region cried out in pain. I don't believe this, she cried. I just don't understand. He'd hit her many times before but this was more extreme than anything previous.

Chapter Four

"You're a mess," Max told her, "so just stay inside."

Michelle's lips were split and swollen, her cheek purple. She didn't have the strength to get out of bed, let alone go outside. Sometime in the early morning she had pulled herself to the bathroom to get a drink of water to moisten her dry mouth. She didn't turn on the light, so she didn't see her battered face. She yearned for the warmth of the bed. Without touching Max she carefully lay on the edge, pulling what covers she could over her. She willed her body to sleep by finally settling her mind in a world of serene meadows profuse with blossoms and fluttering butterflies.

The last four days of Michelle's stay in Florence was spent in the Pension.

"I'm going back to the Pont de Vecchio to pick you up a gold ring before we leave Italy," Max said the afternoon they were to leave. "That should make you feel better." Max's voice held no emotion; no remorse, no apology. As far as he was concerned Michelle had deserved what he gave her.

Michelle spent longer than usual fixing her make-up to cover the remaining bruises. She was stronger now, the rest had done her good. At least he brought me my meals, she told herself while she combed out the tangles in her hair. She had never seen him so angry, so brutal. Max was usually careful how he hit her. This time he didn't seem to care. Michelle was angry, at Max and at herself, for thinking things might be different. Why couldn't she make it different? If she spoke out at all, he reacted. She shook her head at her reflection in the mirror. The thought to escape, to run away kept coming back to her mind. She didn't really want to do that and yet her heart screamed, "Go!"

"Where would I go, Mirror? And what would I use for money? I don't even know how to speak the language." Michelle's head dropped; her heart wept. I don't have many choices, she decided. She was sitting on the bed feeling sorry for herself when Max came back into the room. She watched his every move as he placed his money belt on the dresser, took a small package from his pocket, and withdrew a ring box. He opened it slowly and took the ring out with his baby finger. Her eyes met his, then quickly fell as he approached her. "If you wear it on your finger we won't have to declare it." He handed it to Michelle. When she didn't take it immediately he grasped her right hand and placed it on her ring finger. "Gorgeous, isn't it?" The ring felt foreign on her hand and she wanted to pull it off, but she was too dejected even to do that. How she wished she had the gumption to run, for that is what her heart yearned to do. But everything seemed so hopeless. She was not only a prisoner with her husband, she was a prisoner to her own fears.

Max eyed the ring with obvious pleasure. "It looks beautiful on your hand. You are my beautiful wife," he told her, briefly touching her face with the back of his hand. "You look good today. I'm glad you stayed and rested this week. You look much better." Taking her by the hands he lifted Michelle from the bed. "Come on, let's go for a walk and have dinner on the Plaza. Our train doesn't leave for Lousanne till 8:45. I've already booked our sleepers for the night." Michelle was glad to be getting out of the room. She picked up her purse and walked with him out the door.

Once on the train, the luggage stored in a cupboard, Max sat down on the bench seat in their private sleeper. "Isn't this much better than the stuffy bunk beds?" Michelle nodded. "Come on, relax." Max kicked off his shoes. The train was already moving out of the station. Michelle watched the bright city lights become fewer and fewer until they were finally gone and only sporadic dots could be seen in the darkness. Max leaned over and pulled down the shutters. "Relax, wife," he repeated, patting the seat beside him. "There's nothing to see outside. Here we have the world to ourselves."

With a shudder Michelle sat down. Max eyed her for a minute, was about to say something, then turned his attention to the travel book. "I can't wait to get to Lousanne and Vent. I can remember skiing down the mountains in competitions, winning lots of ribbons. You remember the ribbons. In the box in my closet?"

Michelle willed herself to relax enough to reply. She remembered the tattered-looking ribbons Max found once he had planned this holiday. "It'll be nice for you to revisit some of those places."

"I'm excited." He jumped up, tossing the book on the seat. "Hey, it's too early for bed. Let's go mingle with the hobnobs in the dining room and have a drink. That way we'll be gone when the porter puts down our bed." Michelle cracked a smile when she stood. She was regretting bedtime. Max hadn't touched her since the night he had beat her and she knew her reprieve was over. Max opened the door and Michelle followed him to the dining car. Max ordered coffee for them both which they drank with very little conversation.

Back in their sleeper an hour later the bench seat was now made into a bed. Max took their suitcases from the closet.

"It's a little close in here with the bed made up. You can change in the bathroom; I'll change here." Michelle left her suitcase on the bed while she went to change. When she came back it was already back in the closet and Max was lying in bed thumbing through the train book which was now looking a bit tattered. She stood for a long moment wondering what to do. Max was lying close to the edge so she would have to climb over him to get to the other side. Panic seized her even before she moved. If she felt like a prisoner in this little compartment, she would be even worse between the wall and Max. She gasped. "What are you waiting for, Woman?" Max's tone was crisp but not angry. "You gotta be tired." Michelle climbed in at the foot of the bed, careful to make as little contact as possible. The top bunk had not been lowered on Max's request so that made it a bit easier for Michelle to get under the covers and lay stiffly against the wall. The wall didn't pose a threat.

Max was nearest the night light and Michelle waited for him to turn it off. He was facing her with the book in his hand. She waited. He didn't lower the book or make any comment. Still Michelle waited, panic making her nauseated. She hoped she wouldn't get sick, but the idea of Max putting his hands on her was choking her with fear. Hadn't he told her he was going to make love to her in every country? Hadn't it been several days since he had approached her except for the odd caress and fondling? She lay tight against the cold wall, the train rocking back and forth as it sped down the track in the blackness. The longer she lay, and the longer Max took to start his lovemaking, the harder it was for Michelle not to cry out. She was so relieved when Max turned away, and without a word tossed the book on the floor, and turned out the light. Tears of relief ran freely onto Michelle's pillow.

Michelle awoke first. The clamor of activity and the noise

of the foreign voices frightened her. She was suddenly aware that the train had stopped. "Max! The train has stopped. Are we in Lousanne?"

Max sat up quickly. "Probably." He jumped out of bed. "I wonder why they didn't wake us up. They knew we needed to get off in Lousanne."

They hurried into their clothes. "Wait here," Max instructed leaving the compartment. Michelle finished with her hair and had things packed when Max returned. "We're at a town called Vallorbe. We're going through customs here. The Swiss authorities are coming to check our passports and tickets. They want us cleared before we enter Switzerland and before we leave the train." He rummaged through his money belt retrieving their passports and tickets. "We're only about an hour out of Lousanne."

Before Michelle could make any kind of comment two men dressed in military uniforms stood at their door. In broken English one spoke, "Passports?" Max handed them the two passports. The official looked them over and then stamped Michelle's. Handing it to her, he said, "Madam should carry her own. Should yours become lost, or you become separated, Madam will need hers."

Max tried to snatch the passport. "We won't become separated!"

Michelle clutched the book to her chest. "I can keep it in my purse. Then your pouch won't be so full." Max didn't argue, which surprised Michelle, but she carefully avoided any comment about it once the officials were gone.

As the train began to move again Michelle stood in the aisle outside the compartment watching the sun rise over the Swiss Alps. Their beauty brought tears to her eyes, and a lightness she hadn't experienced before on this trip lifted her spirits. This was God's country. She was filled with a reverent admiration as she stared at the rugged, crisp, white capped mountains which reached into the now blue heavens.

"I wish you'd smile like that more often," Max said. "It makes your face even more beautiful."

"Look at those mountains!" Michelle didn't take her eyes from the scenery. "They look like they are a part of heaven."

Max only glanced fleetingly out the window. "You're part of heaven, Woman. Come here!"

Michelle was so intrigued with the view she didn't pay heed to Max's order. ""It's breathtaking!" Her breathing was rapid with excitement. "I can't wait to get out of here and breathe the mountain air. I can almost taste it."

Max grabbed her by both shoulders and spun her around. Her excitement thrilled him. "Then the sooner we finish our little business, the sooner you'll be off this train. I don't want you to miss the experience of making love to me on the train before we get to Lousanne."

Michelle went weak and her heart sank. Instantly the beauty and exhilaration disappeared. Max's compulsion for sex darkened the beauty of the world around her. How could he cheapen everything?

Max locked the door and drew the curtains closed. "I'm all yours, wife! Undress me!" Michelle stood frozen, her stomach churning. She hoped she wouldn't vomit as she began unbuttoning Max's shirt. Her knees shook and her fingers wouldn't work. As soon as her cool fingers touched his skin, he groaned. Grabbing her hands he pushed her to the bed. "You're too slow, Woman! What are you? A clumsy cow!" It only took a few minutes for Max to be satisfied. With a contented grin, as though everything was kosher, he climbed off the bed, and dressed.

Michelle sucked in a huge lungful of air as soon as she

stepped off the train. It was so crisp and clean it took her breath away. The majestic beauty and immaculate cleanliness of the station was so appealing it took Michelle's mind off the harsh demeaning scene that had taken place just a little while before. Max had gone to the pay phone to call the pension in Interlaken, a few miles up the road, to make sure their reservations were in order. "A taxi is coming for us," he said upon his return. The look he gave her sent ripples up and down her spine, but she could not read its meaning.

Once loaded into the taxi, with the driver talking to Max, Michelle captured everything she saw to put into her memory. She sensed that Switzerland was going to be her favorite part of their holiday. She stored in her mind the stark cleanliness of the whole countryside and the deluge of flowers lining the streets, hanging in wicker baskets on store fronts, and filling display windows. The trees, the mountains, the seemingly unnatural orderliness of the whole area was very appealing. Maybe, she thought, if she had enough of these things stored in her memory, she would be able to block out the degrading sexual moments with Max.

"I don't think I've ever seen you look like this before," Max told her when they had settled into their room at Frau Schmidt's pension. "I'm not sure I like it."

"Like what?" Michelle asked somewhat apologetically.

"I don't know. I just don't think I like it." He pulled himself taller to tower over her slender frame. "Maybe you'd better tell me what you are thinking about." His voice was firm but there was a sense of unsureness in his tone. Michelle was not sure how to deal with it.

"I'm not thinking anything particular. I've just never seen such beauty and cleanliness before. It's almost unreal."

"I don't believe you! Mountains are mountains! You see one, you see them all. It's just repetitious, confining scenery."

Michelle couldn't believe Max didn't see the beauty. "The other countries were different. They all had their own appeal, but this country is alluring. I love the cleanliness, the order, and the beauty. This is heavenly; all the other places were earthy."

"Earthy? What kind of word is that?" He stopped as if thinking of something profound to say that would match her creative word. "You're weird, you know. Italy and France were full of culture. You wouldn't know about that, though, would you? Culture isn't something you appreciate. Scenery," he added, "is okay, but you've blown it all out of proportion."

Michelle did feel a little foolish but no one could take away how she felt. It was as if she had found a little bit of herself.

It was unusually warm for October so Max and Michelle strolled down the ornate streets. Every building displayed the typical Swiss chalets with black or green or brown shutters and window boxes filled with flowers. Shops were laden with watches, beer steins, clocks and mountain equipment. Michelle was intrigued by the number of music boxes and bells. Every store or cafe or restaurant played traditional alpine music and yodeling. Several times Michelle found herself humming an unknown tune she had heard. Her bouncing step kept time with the music.

"Michelle!" Instantly she stopped. Max rarely called her by her name. He had fallen behind. "Are you going to a fire or something?"

"No," she beamed. "I just can't get my heart to settle down. It's bubbling over and governing my feet." She tried to speak seriously.

"Oh, don't be so childish. You're embarrassing me." Michelle glanced around at the empty sidewalk. The angry look on Max's face left her next words unsaid and she slowed her pace to match his. "Let's go have lunch," he said curtly. "I'm hungry and its a long way back to Frau Schmidt's."

The Alpine Meadow Restaurant was dimly lit, making it warm and cozy. Michelle ate enthusiastically while she absorbed the atmosphere and applauded the local musicians who performed traditional selections. Even Max seemed to be softened by the friendliness and courtesy of the waiters and waitresses.

Max and Michelle spent the whole afternoon window shopping and walking through the beautiful parks. They spent several hours in one Swiss clock shop watching the hundreds of decorative time pieces as they ticked the same rhythm, each displaying the same correct time—from grandfather clocks, to mantel clocks, to cuckoo clocks mounted on the wall. Pendulum, electric, and wind-up clocks all running with exactness, ticking and purring. Michelle was fascinated by the little yodellers who on the hour scooted out to sing, or the billy goats that would bump a store keeper every half hour. She laughed at the woman with a rolling pin who chased her husband around the castle she popped out of every time the clock chimed. It was an entertaining sight, one which both Michelle and Max enjoyed. The only purchase Max made was a gold Swiss wrist-watch with Roman numerals.

The sun had set over the Jungfrau, a snow capped peak in the distance, as the Engers made their way back to the pension. They had eaten dinner in a quaint dimly lit restaurant before starting back. The street was lit up with decorative gas lanterns; the ghostly mountains reached through the darkness to penetrate a star spangled sky. Michelle walked with her eyes upward immersing herself in the ambiance of peace. As they entered their bedroom, she shivered openly. Their room was cool and Michelle hugged her arms to her body. "Oh, to climb under that feather tick," she commented to no one. "But I think I'll warm up in the shower first."

"Me too," Max put in.

"Okay," Michelle told him. "You shower first. I'll write on some of these postcards."

"No!" Max snatched the postcards from her hand. "They can wait. We'll shower together. We haven't done that for a long time. Besides," he added with a smirk, "we'll warm up faster."

Michelle's disappointed look went unnoticed. Max was already heading for the bathroom, pulling his sweater over his head.

Interlaken was even more beautiful in the morning. Melodious bells rang in the fresh morning air and drifted away on the soft alpine breeze. Michelle and Max ate a hearty breakfast at Frau Schmidt's before they left for the day. Her fluent English amazed Michelle, and their hostess explained that she had been schooled in England. However, she stated, most Europeans spoke English as a second language.

From Interlaken the Engers boarded a train on a small gauge railroad that would take them to the tiny mountain community of Grindlewald. Since Grindlewald lay halfway up the mountain, the train pulled slow and hard around the lake and up the steep incline. When they and the other passengers stepped out at the station, both Max and Michelle took a second to catch their breath. Michelle spoke first. "Look at these homes. They are so enchanting! I wonder if these are their normal style of houses or do they do it for the tourists?"

"This is normal," said a voice close to Michelle. "They're built like this because of the terrain and the heavy amounts of snow in winter, but mostly, the Swiss people just love simple beauty."

Michelle stood open-mouthed. Standing beside her was a familiar looking face but she could not remember where she had seen it. Max showed no signs of recognition. "I'm Peter Zimmer," the man introduced himself in impeccable English.

"You're not Swiss," Max said, more a comment than a question.

"No, I am from the great US of A. I just dress for the occasion," he said noticing Max's full body surveillance of his wearing apparel. Not bothered by it he added with a crooked grin, "I say when in Rome, do as the Romans." Michelle liked the leather hiking boots, the red and black flannel shirt and the leather knee-length shorts. On his head he wore a green Robin Hood type of cap with a pheasant feather stuck in the band. He held a wooden hiking staff in his hand. "You will find," Peter continued, "that you are the odd people here. Everyone, native or tourist, dresses like this. It is more functional."

Michelle smiled at his easy demeanor. "This place looks like a scene from the book, *Heidi*."

Peter Zimmer gestured with his arm. "This is the home of Heidi. This is where the story originated."

"I'm impressed," Michelle said as she took another look around.

"Well, I'm off," Peter told them. "My holiday is over for another week. So long comrades."

"Good-bye," Michelle said with a small wave.

"You were sure friendly," Max chided taking Michelle by the hand and pulling her further up the narrow cobblestone path.

Michelle slipped on the steep incline.

Max jerked her arm. "Don't do it again. You knew nothing about him. Who knows what he was after."

They stopped at the top of the path where it split into two paths. "D-Didn't he seem a bit familiar?" she hesitantly asked.

"No! So don't try to justify your behavior with that excuse." He began pulling her along the path again and only stopped when a farmer with a wagon load of manure crossed their path. Together they watched him drive into the field where he began shoveling the fertilizer onto the green pasture. The farmer waved to them and Max gave him a little back-hand wave before striding away from Michelle. Michelle smiled at the farmer then followed her husband. She lagged behind taking in the beauty of the flora and enjoying the calmness and serenity of the walk. Even Max seemed preoccupied with the surroundings. He stopped for a second to wait for Michelle to catch up. He took hold of her hand. "Let's take the path through the trees to see where it goes." The path, still made of reddish-brown cobblestone had been worn smooth by lots of feet. Michelle could see it disappear into the trees just a short distance ahead.

"Okay," she said, wondering what magic scene they would encounter as they walked. As they entered the forest Michelle could see the corner of a large brown building and hear a motor struggling as if under lots of strain. As they got closer she could see a large cable and then a chairlift leave the building and rise above the trees. People were leaving the building laden with baskets and boxes. Most were dressed in traditional alpine costumes, and a few were noticeably tourists dressed as Max and Michelle.

Max picked up a pamphlet from a nearby rack just inside the building. Michelle glanced at it over his shoulder and the words, "longest chairlift" caught her attention. "This is The First," Max read. "It is the longest chairlift in the world, going up the mountain in four different stages." He looked at his wife. "Sounds interesting. This is used as a tourist attraction, but it says that this is the only mode of transportation for the locals to use to get to their homes all the way up the mountain. I'm going up."

"All the way?" Michelle asked with some trepidation.

"Of course." His response was emphatic.

"I-I'm not sure I-I..."

"You either come with me or stay here by yourself." Before she could say anything he gave it a second thought. "No way, you will come with me. I am not leaving you alone." Again as many times before, Max grabbed her hand and pulled her to the line of people who were already waiting for the lift.

"I don't mind waiting for you here. You know I struggle with heights." Michelle tried to speak softly to keep the conversation private.

"These people use this lift every day, coming and going. What are you, some sissy?"

Michelle's heart raced. They were only two people away from getting on. The benches looked bare and insecure. Nothing but a tiny bar held a person on the wooden bench. She watched as two people sitting on a bench were lifted off the ground. Immediately her feet went numb and tingly. She watched it rise above the trees and into the blue sky, a razorback mountain a short distance away. Suddenly her fear diminished and a wave of excitement swelled in her. It would take her to the top of the world, on top of all this majesty. Max didn't miss the change of expression on Michelle's face. "I'll come," she told him not taking her eyes off the mountain.

Max didn't have time to comment. An attendant helped them onto the bench and dropped the support bar in front of them. With a heart-stopping jolt, the chair lifted off. Immediately Michelle's bravery wavered. Her feet suddenly went cold and she found it hard to catch her breath. They bounced out of the exit and in the next second were high above the trees slowly moving upward. Max was talking about the amount of money this ride must make every day, but Michelle was trying to replace her fear with the sights and sounds of the surroundings. The pine scent filled her nostrils and the ringing and clanging of the cow bells and the feeling of rising higher and higher soon left her fear far behind. She was rising above it, giving her an exhilaration she could hardly keep to herself.

"Don't jiggle the chair!" Max growled. His face was much whiter than before they left the building. "This ride isn't frightening."

Max's accusation brought Michelle back to reality. "I'm not scared," she simply told him.

"Then sit still." Max seemed agitated so Michelle tried to hold her emotions in check. Only her eyes showed the enjoyment she was feeling.

Shortly they stopped and stepped down. Following the throng of people the few feet to lift number two, Michelle hesitated. Without looking at her husband she said cautiously, "Max, I'd like to walk back down the mountain from here."

"I thought you weren't scared!" Max kept on walking and Michelle hurried to keep up.

"I'm not afraid. In fact I feel wonderful. I just want to take the walking path down so I can soak this all up." They were at the second lift now. "Please Max. I love it here."

Before Max could protest, the attendant gently guided Max to the bench seat. "Madam?" he said anxiously holding his hand out to her.

Michelle stepped out of the line. With a wave of her arm, she called, "I'll see you at the bottom." Max had no option but to go up, his face red with fury.

Michelle watched him for a minute, her guilt and fear of reprisal quickly disappearing. She would deal with those later. Right now she was on her own. Taking a deep breath she began her descent to the bottom. Not knowing exactly where to go she just stayed on the path and followed it down as it wound through the forest and up and down the hills. Any fear she had of Max's possible reaction she pushed to the back of her mind.

This was the present and she wanted to enjoy every minute of it. For a while the trees were so dense the panoramic view was blocked from sight. Squirrels scurried back and forth along the path, and at one point Michelle startled a young deer with her movements. Her lighthearted steps only faltered once when she heard male voices approaching her. She wanted to run and hide but chastising herself for her fears, she slowed her pace and allowed the two men to pass. "Ma'amselle," they greeted and continued on their way.

Michelle felt such an overwhelming sense of freedom and self-fulfillment as she walked, that she almost didn't see the building to the right of the path. It was the same building the first chairlift had left from. She continued walking down the more familiar path until she had reached the train station. Going inside she found an empty booth and ordered an iced tea. She had enough change for that. For a moment at least she felt like a free and competent adult. Then she spotted the pay phone on the wall. Why not? she told herself. Max wouldn't know that she had phoned the girls until he got back to Canada. With a sweep of anticipation Michelle went to the phone and dialled the operator. After giving her the calling card number she waited while the connection went through. Michelle had never felt such anticipation. She heard the phone being picked up on the other end of the line. Without waiting she said, "Sonja?"

"Mom?" Sonja replied. "Hey, Anna! It's Mom! How are you, Mom? Are you having a good time? Where are you?"

"Hey, one question at a time," Michelle laughed. "I'm fine. We're in a little Swiss town that looks like a story book picture. In fact, this town is the origin of the little girl Heidi"

"It's good to hear from you. We've been waiting. By the way what time is it there?"

Michelle looked at her watch. "Oh dear, it's three thirty.

That means its..."

Sonja chuckled. "It's okay. Anna has been in bed since ten and I'm going shortly. It's after midnight now but I had homework to do. Here, Anna wants to say hi."

Michelle waited for the exchange then heard Anna speak. "Hi, Mom."

"Hello, honey. How's school?"

"I miss you Mom but college is great. I love it here."

"That's good. I just want you to be happy. I can't talk long but I wanted to hear your voices." She had to stop to control the sniffles that might give away the homesickness she felt.

"Are you okay," Anna asked not missing the quiver in Michelle's voice.

"I'm fine and there's lots of neat things here. I've got tons of postcards to bring home. Your Dad let's..." That was as far as Michelle got. The phone was snatched from her hand and harshly replaced. Michelle gasped as she heard Anna exclaim, "Mama?"

"You're nuts, Woman!" Max shouted. Guests in the restaurant stopped and the room suddenly became silent.

"I was just talking to the girls," she cowered. "I didn't think there was any harm in that."

Max pulled her out onto the street. "You're very devious aren't you?" His grip tightened. "You must have planned this all day."

"Oh, Max," Michelle tried to explain. "I just wanted to share this experience with the girls. Don't you wish you could share it with them?"

"That's rubbish. You're supposed to be sharing it with me, remember?" Michelle tried to squirm out of his grip, but it tightened so much that Michelle felt like passing out. "Somehow," Max snorted, "you have forgotten."

Again Michelle found herself being propelled down the

street. Finally when Max realized he wasn't going anywhere in particular, he stopped. They were now standing in front of an ice cream shop. He pushed her inside and shoved her into the nearest empty booth. "You have me baffled, Woman. You are not the same wife I left Canada with. You've forgotten your place and I am losing control of you." He grabbed her wrist. "Women are supposed to be controlled."

"Who made those rules?" she asked and then immediately bit her tongue as if to retract the question.

"Men who don't tolerate insubordinate lippy wives," Max hissed across the table. Michelle slumped back out of his reach, snatching her wrist from his grasp.

The waiter came and Max ordered a coffee and a roll but made no gesture to order anything for Michelle. "Madam?" the waiter asked. Michelle shook her head.

Michelle sat quietly as Max finished his coffee and roll. Once outside, he took her by the hand, his hold less restraining. "I like you when you're quiet, Wife, but don't pout. It's not becoming to your beautiful face." Michelle allowed herself to be taken in and out of shops laden with tartans, more clocks and music boxes. When it finally got dark and they were riding the train back to Frau Schmidt's in Interlaken, Michelle began to wonder about her girls. What on earth would they be thinking? Hopefully they would think she'd been cut off and then they wouldn't worry. They couldn't return the call because they didn't know from what place their mother was calling.

Max did not refer again to the happenings of the day for which Michelle was grateful. It was almost like his domination was a natural protocol and she should just accept it. Well, that's not surprising. She'd accepted it for twenty-four years. Michelle couldn't understand what had come over her since they had arrived in Europe. Her occasional assertiveness was so unlike her. Perhaps she had accepted his behavior so long that something inside her was openly rebelling. Maybe it was the setting or the fact they were away from home. Well, whatever it was, Michelle told herself, she'd better get any notions of change out of her mind or she would be in big trouble.

Chapter Five

Michelle could have wept when the train pulled up the mountain and Interlaken slowly passed by the window. She couldn't believe how the days had slipped past and they were leaving an area she had come to love.

Max already had his schedule book open and was engrossed in the things he was reading. A lump filled Michelle's throat with the same feelings of abandonment as when they left their girls in Canada. Interlaken, Grindlewald and the Jungfrau were places she would never forget. She closed her eyes to deepen the impression of the memory she had felt there.

When Michelle finally opened her eyes, the train was speeding down the track. They were now out of the deepest mountains and the smooth ride was lulling. When she looked at Max and found him dozing, she carefully removed her walkman from her bag and snapped in one of the Swiss tapes Max had allowed her to buy. As soon as the music seeped into the earphones, Michelle leaned back, her head against the window as she watched the endless ranges of mountains rush by.

They changed trains in Luzern, had an hour stop in Zurich, then entered Austria. Much to Michelle's surprise and excitement, the countryside looked much like that of Switzerland. The contours of the area seemed softer and not as sharp as in Switzerland, but the appeal much the same because of the mountains, trees and flowers.

A hotel booking agent in Innsbruck had reserved a room at the Pension Aberbrun for Max and Michelle, so they took time to eat dinner before finding their way to their hotel in the darkness. Michelle's heart jumped and she felt a wave of guilt sweep over her when she followed Max into the room. The room was furnished with two of the nicest looking twin beds Michelle had ever seen. Maybe it was the turquoise blue eiderdown comforters that appealed to her, but no, Michelle knew it was because the beds were far too small for two people. They were singles.

He must have read her looks, for Max sneered, "Appealing to you, isn't it?" When she didn't answer he added, "Don't deny your pleasure at the sleeping accommodations. It shows on your face." Max turned away from her and Michelle approached one of the beds cautiously. She sat on the edge and removed her shoes. Max placed one of the large suitcases on the other bed, then tossed the smaller one next to it.

"We'll only dirty one set of sheets," he gloated. "That'll give'em something to talk about when they make up the room in the mornings."

Hardness filled Michelle's chest, and the disgust she felt was now accompanied by anger. She struggled hard not to tell Max how she felt. They would be terribly cramped trying to sleep in such a small bed.

Max was already undressing for bed as Michelle sat stunned trying to get her mind to relax and replace her unpleasant thoughts of sleeping so closely to Max. No matter how hard she tried, nothing would cover up the intensity that was building inside of her. Michelle reminded herself that it was late, morning would come as it always did and then they would be out in public where she could add more sights and sounds to her mind.

Later, when Max lay next to her in the crowded bed, his hands roughly fondling her, she let her mind drift, and thankfully she was able to slip away where all sense of physical feeling stopped.

An oppressive sensation woke Michelle the next morning. With Max's arm lying heavily across her tummy, she realized she had not moved all night. Squirming until he lifted his head from her shoulder, Michelle found herself stiff and sore. In the confined space of the bed she could only turn one way and that was on her side facing her husband. At first she hesitated but the pain in her body was unbearable. She twisted, hoping not to wake him. If she could just lie on her side for a moment. Once the pain subsided she would roll back. She would like to have gotten up but that would have awakened him. At least when he was asleep, she was alone. Her naked body could not help touching his, and instantly Michelle felt Max's hand press in on the lower part of her back.

"Mm, that's better." Max's breath warmed Michelle's closed eyelids. "I like it when a woman wakes me with soft touches of her body."

Immediately Michelle tried to turn back and pull away. Max pressed her hard to him. "Oh, no you don't." His voice was soft but sharp. "I like you this way, face-to-face, naked, warm... You do wonderful things to me." His hands caressed her lightly and she stiffened under his touch.

"Don't tighten up on me, Wife." Max's voice was louder. "I made love to a board last night. I want this morning to be different."

The feeling of disgust made Michelle nauseous and she thought she would be sick. The feeling was so great she started to struggle. Max pinned her against the wall. Michelle's anger gave her strength and for the first time in her life she began to wrestle against Max's aggressiveness. For a second Max seemed surprised. Then noticing the determined look on his wife's face, he shoved her hard onto the pillow and threw his body onto hers to restrain her movements. Fury lit her face and she tried to push him off. Max stared down at her, pinning her arms above her head. Then he sat on her.

"What do you think you are doing, Woman? You're wild!"

Michelle's pent up emotions overflowed. "Get off me, you animal!"

A look almost like fear crossed Max's face and instantly he reacted in the only way he knew how. He held her tighter. She had never acted like this before. He couldn't imagine why she was doing this now.

"Get off me!" Michelle protested again and gave her body a heave.

Max was too strong to move. He tried to clamp his mouth over hers to quiet her. Michelle turned her head and the kiss caught her on the chin. He swore as his lip began to bleed and before Michelle could speak, Max had retaliated with a blow to the side of her face. Michelle saw stars and for a minute could not breathe.

All fell quiet, and Max slowly stretched his large body over his wife's prone silent one. "You're mine," he whispered hoarsely. "Don't ever forget it." He licked his lips, his eyes never leaving Michelle's face when he moved to lie beside her. Her body was no longer rigid and hard but lay soft and supple under his touch. Her look never changed; her body never moved. She lay as if in a trance, her spirit spent. Max's hands caressed her but his desire and thoughts were no longer on his physical needs. "Let's go sightseeing," he said as if nothing had happened. "I want to look at some old ski hills I remember skiing as a kid." Michelle turned slightly to watch Max go into the bathroom. She slowly climbed out of bed, far too weak even to cry.

"I spent a lot of time in this area as a school boy," Max told her once they had eaten and were walking down a country road. "I bet I've skied every trail. You'll find the pubs and homes quite different to the ones in Switzerland. These are quaint and old, far more homey."

The stoic look Michelle gave him, he construed as submissiveness. So feeling more in control, he continued, "You can buy some souvenirs for the kids and I'll pay for them. And I will show you where I won my first skiing medal. I was number one for over five years." They walked further down the road until they reached a little country pub that displayed a bus sign. "Here is where we catch the bus," he told her. Within minutes the bus rattled to a stop. "Oh wonderful!" Max complained. "A war veteran. It'll take us all day."

Michelle didn't see any war veteran. But just before she was going to speak she realized Max wasn't talking about a person but about the bus. It did look a bit old. "Oh well, we'll just enjoy the scenery," Michelle said as they climbed aboard.

"One mountain looks like all the rest. You see one, you see them all." Max took his novel out of his pocket as soon as he sat down. Michelle couldn't imagine anyone being born in this wonderful setting and not liking the mountains. She couldn't understand how someone could not see their beauty or, she decided, someone who wouldn't *admit* he saw their beauty.

Once the bus was on its way and Max was involved in his book, Michelle took the time to think. She had to go over in her mind just what had happened this morning. She had no idea what was coming over her. Never had she been so vocal with Max. Never had she ever reacted to him like that. What made her do so today? And so aggressively! She glanced at Max almost feeling exposed as she thought. Her mind was so active she wondered if Max could hear her thoughts. When she realized he was paying her no attention, she let herself think some more. Her feelings were jumbled and confused. She didn't even know quite how to sort them all out. Max's blow was still burning, emotionally, although the actual pain was gone. She had probably deserved that. Her own anger had led him to it. But, somewhere deep inside, a little voice told her that she had done nothing that deserved physical abuse. Her mind went back to the many times he had hit her before and the many times he had struck at Billy. Those blows hurt Michelle more than the ones that landed on her. She remembered taking the blame so Max would hit her instead of Billy. For some reason he never hit the girls. Of course, Sonja was his favorite and Anna was a little pest, someone you totally ignore. Brush it off from time to time and it would go away.

So why did Max have to strike out. Frustration! That must be the problem. Like today, he was frustrated because she lashed out at him. Michelle had never seen that look of anger on his face before. It seemed that not only was she changing, but so was he, and she was afraid of both outcomes. What could she do to be prepared for the weeks ahead? Michelle tried thinking back to her actions and what had triggered Max's increased anger and aggression. Surely a dip in the Mediterranean shouldn't have made him angry. She wasn't doing anything wrong. He allowed her to listen to her tapedeck, but he still had that fierce disgusted look when she wore it. Meeting and talking to the stranger in Florence? That had been a big problem. Wasn't she to speak to anyone but her husband?

The bus hit a pothole and everything bounced. Max said something under his breath but didn't even look up. Michelle thought about the changes she was feeling emotionally. There was something different. It began when she played her walkman on the plane and felt her children close to her, even if Max wasn't pleased. Going for the swim when Max wasn't able to stay in the water, riding the chairlift for the first time, then walking down the path in Grindlewald by herself and acknowledging the greeting made by the fellow hikers. Finally speaking to the girls, just dialing the number, speaking to the operator, and talking. Even having the money to buy the iced tea. Now, as she sat looking across at Max she knew what had made her react so aggressively. It was a feeling, though inadequate as yet, of independence and freedom. Was she wrong to want these feelings? This she didn't know. How she wished she had someone she could talk to. But there was no one, she decided. Knowing this now, she understood why Max was reacting. He sensed her feeling of independence and it was a threat to him. So, every time she did something that even hinted at being more independent, Max would try to stop it with force, the only thing he knew. Power, force and control. Now Michelle could see things a little more clearly and everything began to make more sense. At home she was in his domain with his rules. Out here, where he didn't have as much control, he felt helpless. Michelle was the only thing he could control, and he felt smaller if he couldn't.

Somehow Michelle felt relieved. As she looked at Max she felt sorry for him. She could feel her emotions surfacing and tears stinging in her eyes: twenty-four years of marriage under a dictator's thumb and the loss of her individuality. She almost cried aloud when she thought of the fear Max must have felt every time he sensed she might be expressing this tiny bit of independence to try to stand up for her own needs and desires. Surely I'm allowed some, she told herself. Should I always be under his thumb? Always be dominated? Should someone else do my thinking for me? Why can't I fulfill some of my own wants? Max does? Am I any different from him?

Michelle was suddenly amazed. Why hadn't she thought

of this before? Why couldn't she have thought of this years sooner so they both could have adjusted more easily? It would be a nightmare for her to try to assert more independence now. She knew well how angry he got over the little things. She shuddered openly.

"Cold?" Max asked, "or afraid?"

Michelle jumped at the tone of his voice. "W-why should I be afraid?"

"You were so intent on the passing scenery I thought you were afraid of falling into the gorge below us." Michelle noticed the plunging cliffs and the waterfall flowing into the river in the valley below. "It's beautiful! It's absolutely breathtaking!"

"If you didn't see the gorge, what were you so engrossed in? I actually spoke to you a couple of times." Michelle reddened. Max continued, watching her expression closely. "I've seen you disappear on me when you are listening to your music but to go that far all on your own... It must have been something big." His voice rose as he spoke.

Michelle's lips quivered and Max grabbed her, twisting her to face him. "Tell me what your devious little mind was concocting now." Michelle looked helplessly around her and was surprised to see that she and Max were the only passengers. She hadn't even been aware that the bus had made numerous stops. "That's right!" he laughed. "We're alone, so you can speak up."

Michelle squirmed out of his loosening grip and slid closer to the window. For a moment she wished she could jump out and run. Then for a moment she desired to tell him how she felt. What could he do? Hit her? She'd lived through that before. He couldn't hurt her any more than that, could he? Especially not on the bus? Max wouldn't resort to anything more nasty as long as they were in public, and the bus driver counted as public.

"Max?" Michelle started hesitantly. "I-I-I want to apologize for my outburst this morning. I shouldn't have done it."

"Then you know you deserved the smack I gave you?" His chest swelled and for a second Michelle felt herself withdraw.

"No," she said abruptly not waiting for fear to make her stop. "Nothing warrants physical abuse."

Max was taken back. "Why you little..."

"You can hit me if you want Max, but I am going to tell you how I feel. I know..." He was glaring at her. "I know you don't think I have any feelings and that I'm not worth anything. So did I. However, I was wrong and so are you. As I walked down that mountain at Grindlewald I felt something locked up inside of me screaming to get out. It was me." Her voice was getting louder to match her feelings and she made herself speak more softly.

"That's ridiculous, Wife. You are you. I've made you the woman you are." He stopped. "I knew I should have made you ride that chairlift with me."

"You had no other choice at the time," Michelle told him. "Not that I had planned it. It just worked out that way once I decided to follow my feelings. And I really needed that walk."

"For what? To go man hunting?" His shriek made the bus driver look up at them through his mirror.

"I was waiting for you at the bottom, remember? You must have started down right after that lift finished its second level."

"You weren't waiting for me. You were on the phone!"

"So I didn't have time for a rendezvous. And besides, I thought you would be happy knowing the girls were doing okay. They are yours too, you know."

"So you keep telling me. Anyway," his tone a little lower, "that does not give you reason for your behavior in bed this morning. You've never done it before but for some reason since we left home, you've decided to override any of my authority."

"Don't you think I have any right to say whether I want sex or not? Don't my needs count? In anything?"

"I've never thought about it!" He stopped. He had no idea what was going on. "Anyway you've never made an issue of it before."

"Well, I was wrong. I am now." Michelle was surprised at herself. "I don't want this to separate us, Max. Just give me some breathing room."

"Breathing room!" His voice raised again. "What do you mean, breathing room? What do you think this expensive holiday is?"

"Max. It's nothing to get angry about. I just need a little spa..."

Max grabbed her and gave her a hard shake. "I should have kept you harnessed at home. I give you everything and now you want more. You are mine. I made you what you are and that's how I like you. It has taken over twenty years to train you to be the perfect wife."

Michelle's shoulders cried out in pain as the bus stopped and Max let her go. The driver eyed them as they stepped down onto the sidewalk. Max gave him a dirty look and grasped Michelle's arm before she could move. "Stay right beside me, Woman! I don't want you to get any more bright ideas and embarrass me in front of anyone. Not even a bus driver!"

"Have I ever been the embarrassing one in public," she retorted in a hoarse whisper.

"Don't push me too far, Wife. I'm still boss in this household. Don't forget it!"

Michelle pulled on him until he stopped. "Please Max. I want us to get through the rest of this holiday. Please try to understand. I just need a bit of space."

"I don't think you have any idea what you're talking

72

about. I've made you what you are today. You'd still be that little colonial girl I married if it hadn't been for me."

"Just a little breathing space, please." Michelle dropped her head, knowing her pleas were futile, but she clung to a thread of hope now that her feelings were out in the open.

"Come on, I need a drink." Max pulled her along the stone street, over a bridge that joined two steep hills, and down a path to a little coffee house. "If you want us to get through the rest of this holiday as you said you did, then don't cause me any more trouble. Just do as you're told, and if you need this so- called breathing space, we'll do it together. I love relaxing with you."

Michelle didn't say anything. The waiter took their order as soon as they were seated. It didn't take him long to hand Michelle a steaming mug of coffee which she cupped in both her hands to sip its warmth. She shut out all unpleasant thoughts and focused her attention on her surroundings.

She and Max were the only patrons in the low-ceilinged room. Everything was decorated in shiny glistening wood, and red and black checked gingham. Even the ties holding back the curtains and the table covers had the gingham. It was set off by red candle holders and tiny red bows. The dimly lit room made the atmosphere warm and homey.

As Max and Michelle left the building they stopped to let a farmer herd his half dozen head of cattle into a barn right on the edge of the road next to the coffee house. The farmer smiled at the tourists and continued with his chores.

"Fascinating," said Michelle, "Imagine having a farm on main street."

"These people live differently than we do," Max chastised.

"I know. I wasn't judging them. In fact I think this whole village is a lovely place. I'd like to know what keeps people here when there doesn't seem to be any means of making a liveli-hood. There's no industry or anything."

"Let me show you." Max gleamed. He was in control again. "I told you I have spent a lot of time here."

"But that was ski season."

Max led her to a path that switch-backed up the side of the mountain. They followed it until they reached the summit. Max stopped abruptly. Below them lay a scattering of tumbled-down buildings and an abandoned ski lift. "I don't believe this. It's all gone. This was a really good business when I was growing up and it was always busy. I wonder why it wasn't kept up." Max's disappointment seemed to anger him. "Let's go ask," he said stomping back down the path they had just walked up.

"Aren't we going to at least look around?"

"Hurry up Woman," he ordered as if time would alter the changes to the past. They were almost running when they reached the bottom. For the first time Max took a good look at the village. "I don't believe this," he repeated in dismay. "Even the rental shop is closed and so is the little restaurant near the bridge. We always got to sleep in the attic on straw beds. Hey!" he called to a passing man. "What's happened to this place?"

The man looked startled. "Sir?" he asked in accented English.

"When did this town die?" Max's voice was stern and cold as if this solitary man had been responsible for the disappear-ance of Max's childhood nostalgia.

"Time changes all life," the man told him. "Bigger and better things are closer to the larger cities. It is more econom-ical to go there."

"But this was such a popular place when I was a boy," Max's voice trailed in resignation to the reality of it all. "I won medals here. I made friends here."

The local man had started to walk away then stopped. "This was not a real tourist center. This little recreation," he pointed up at the abandoned ski hill, "was operated by a local family. Medals and ribbons won were supplied by the village merchants. It was no big deal. When the Visser's grew too old to run the old manual lift, the ski hill closed down. That is all."

"You must be mistaken. This was always busy. It was very popular."

"Only for families of villagers and close friends. Nothing more." The man walked away with a brief nod and smile to the Engers. Max stood transfixed. He didn't believe that his ski medals had been anything but sensational. They couldn't have been just some local handout. "Peasant!" he called out after the man.

"Max!" Michelle was astounded. "He must know. He lives here."

"Calling me a liar, Woman?" Max stomped off toward the bus stop, pulling on Michelle's arm as he walked.

"Of course not. It's just that things seem so much bigger and more important when you are a child. And nothing in this world ever stays the same." She tried to keep her voice calm, so as not to aggravate him even though her mind was telling him to shut-up.

The return bus ride should have been considerably shorter because there were only two other passengers, so less stops. Yet, the ride seemed endless and to make matters worse they had a lengthy lay over in Ozadhl before they could catch the express back to Innsbruck.

"This day sure didn't go as I planned it," Max pouted once they were back at their pension. "In fact this whole trip has been a fizzle. What a waste of money."

Michelle would have liked to have commented but

decided to keep her words to herself. When Max was in this mood anything she would say would only give him reason to go into a rampage. And she didn't want that. "Let's dress up and find a really nice place to dine and dance. You enjoy that."

"Humph," Max said, flopping on the edge of the bed. He jerked open his train book and began to read. Michelle went to the suitcase and pulled out the dress Max had bought her in France. It wasn't as wrinkled as she thought it would be, so she hung it up and ran her hand down it several times to smooth out what creases there were."Okay," Max slammed down the book. "Let's go out. It's dinner time anyway."

Michelle took special care in getting ready. She wanted to look her best. Dressed only in her slip when she left the bathroom to get her new dress, she tried to ignore Max's wolfish look as she passed him. Just as she went to reach for her dress she felt his hands fondle her thick brown hair that fell past her shoulders. "You are so beautiful," he said, sliding his arms around her waist to pull her back against him. Automatically Michelle stiffened and he strained her closer. "I want to make love to you before we go." He pressed his lips on the back of her neck and then turned her. Without lifting his mouth he followed the sleek line of her collar bone up the soft supple skin of her neck to place his lips firmly on her mouth. He pressed her to him and Michelle could feel her body and soul want to slash out at him. It took all her strength and mental capacities to turn off the disgust and nausea so she could try to respond to his advances. There's no reason, she reprimanded herself, not to let him have what he wanted. And it just might appease his anger.

Fantasizing as was her habit, Michelle let herself be manipulated to the bed where Max removed her clothes and then his. Michelle allowed Max his pleasure.

Chapter Six

"Can't sleep forever," laughed Max as he flipped the sheets back to uncover Michelle. Max was already dressed in his best suit, his black hair sleek and shiny, his mustache trimmed and waxed. Michelle shivered in the cool air. "If you hurry we'll make the last dance," he told her. "Our fun took longer than I expected."

Michelle looked at the clock as she made her way to the bathroom. Nine o'clock! It was bedtime, not party time. However her stomach told her she had not had much to eat all day so she hurried to dress.

"Your body always makes me feel better, Wife." Max ran his hands up and down her back as they waltzed around the dance floor. "I could stay here all night."

Michelle let him maneuver her around the small dancing area, his movements becoming more and more pronounced. Their meal, which Max had told the waiter to surprise them with, was superb; the wine, the best. Max had polished off most of the bottle by the time they had eaten and Michelle could see the affects it was having on him. His laughs were more boisterous, his actions more extreme. Max spun her around and around till her head was dizzy. She was grateful when he finally took time out to sit and have another drink. By the time he had finished the second bottle Max had made a spectacle of himself in front of the patrons sitting near them with his conversation about being Canada's first billionaire when his ship comes in. When he mentioned their upcoming excursion to Salzburg, Michelle took notice. For the first time in days she felt a surge of excitement. Salzburg, the home of The Sound of Music. In her mind's eye she could see Julie Andrews and Christopher Plummer spinning around on the dance floor and walking in the cool evening in the back garden of the palace. I will look forward to that day, she told herself.

Back on the dance floor, Max was becoming louder and louder and his requests to the band were for faster more livelier music. He was more and more boisterous and obnoxious. It was Max who decided to leave when he noticed they were the only ones in the room except for the orchestra, and they did not appear happy. Even the waiters were standing in the doorways with towels over their arms waiting for these last patrons to leave. "Come on, Wife. Let's take this party somewhere else! Everyone has died here including the music!" Once out on the street Max continued his barrage of criticism. "Looks like the whole town is dead!" he called out as if to announce it to the whole street. "What's a guy to do? I wanna party!"

"Max, let's go back to the hotel. It's 2:00 a.m." She touched his arm.

"What?" he yelled.

"Let's go back. You've had too much to drink." She gave his shirtsleeve a little tug.

He snatched it away so sharply Michelle stumbled. Max grabbed at her, stopping her fall but also catching her by her long hair. "Oh, you wanna party in our hotel room?" He paid no heed to the fact that he had her by the hair. "Well I guess one party is as good as another." He started down the sidewalk, his hand still entangled in Michelle's hair.

"Max?" Tears were running down Michelle's cheek now.

"Changing your mind, Woman?" Max stopped short of the hotel entrance. He let go of her hair as if he had not noticed that he'd even had it. "That's normal." He pulled open the large wooden door. "It was your idea, so party we shall!" He pushed her into the room once he had unlocked it. Max didn't miss the shiver that ran over her as he locked the door including the deadbolt. Fear gripped at Michelle and she froze where she stood. "Excited?" Max asked, his tone as sarcastic as usual. "I'm glad. This is your party so you should be." He glowered at her rigidly, a Cheshire grin lighting his glaring eyes. "Where do we start...?" his slobbery hands already unbuckling Michelle's belt.

As if in self defense Michelle brushed his hands away. Max gripped her by the shoulders. "Don't play games, Wife. This was your idea!"

"Max?" Michelle took a step away.

The back hand blow caught Michelle on the cheek and she fell against the bed. "Max!" Max hit her again and she slid to the floor.

"You're going to party whether you like it or not!" Dropping down beside her he grabbed at the collar of her dress and tore it. "Independence! Breathing space! I'll give you breathing space all right!" Max ripped the material more, his nails tearing her skin as he did. At first Michelle was too stunned to move, then she began to fight back.

"No Max!" she begged. Her cries were silenced by another blow to her face, but she strained to push his weight off her. One of Max's arms was holding hers, the other was angrily ripping her new dress. She managed to free a hand and push him off.

"You're mine! Don't you ever do that again." He hit her hard this time and for a second Michelle felt nothing. When her head cleared slightly she could see Max standing by the bed removing his clothes. With a groan she rolled to her side and tried to get up. The last thing she remembered before his fist caught her chin was the fiery daggers being thrown from his eyes. She knew she was in trouble as she blacked out.

The room was filled with an ashen blue paleness when Michelle came to. Her head ached and her face felt huge and puffy. For a moment she had no recollection of where she was. Her body felt confined and restricted when she moved. She rested momentarily, trying to regain her senses when she slowly became aware of the heavy breathing close to her. Turning slightly she could see Max sprawled on the floor next to her the feather tick half on him and half on the bed. The movement of Michelle's body made her wretch and she knew she was going to be sick. She lay still until the feeling passed, then she began to wiggle herself out of her torn clothes. Every move sent searing pain through her arms, legs and head, but it was her stomach that burned like hot knives being thrust into her. Stopping often it took her a long time to get rid of the rags of her dress that had her bound. Many times she would look at Max and hold her breath for fear he would wake up. Finally she was free and able to move. She had no idea what to do but her whole soul screamed to escape.

As quickly as her battered body would let her, she dressed. It wasn't until she looked in the mirror that she real-ized the extent of her visible injuries. She drew a hand over the black-purplish welt on her face and chin and washed off the blood around her mouth. Her one eye was nearly swollen shut and her neck and shoulders were streaked with red welts. The scratches on her chest and shoulders stung as she washed, but the pain in her stomach and lower abdomen was the worst. She battled the nausea continually. She had to sit on the toilet and lower her head several times before she could continue getting dressed. Still the voice inside her hurried her along. "Get out!

Get out!" it said over and over.

It was seven o'clock when Michelle left the bathroom. Max was in a deep sleep, his snores so quiet Michelle had to keep an eye on him for fear he would wake up. She had no idea what she would do if he did, but she didn't take time to think about it. All she wanted to do was go.

She packed the small suitcase and checked her purse for her passport. She didn't forget the money Max had given her for safe keeping or her rail ticket that he kept in his money pouch. On the night table was the handful of Austrian money Max had changed, so Michelle grabbed it as well. As carefully and quietly as she could she turned the lock and then the deadbolt. Grabbing her jacket and carry-on bag, she quietly left the room. Leaving the perfume, the ring, and the clothes she had purchased, Michelle hurried as fast as she could out of the hotel. She was terrified. She kept looking back over her shoulder, and she had to keep breathing deeply to keep the nausea from erupting. Maybe she should have left a note. No, her absence would tell Max she was gone. Michelle moved as fast as she could to the train station. She knew people were staring at her battered face and poor posture but she didn't care. She knew she had to get as far away as she could.

"Madam?" the ticket agent asked and Michelle realized she had to make a quick decision as to where to go.

Only one word came to mind. "Salzburg," she said. "Yes, Salzburg." Showing her rail pass he pointed to a gate further down the platform. "Thank you," she told him politely. Her eyes darted back and forth expecting to see Max any time, any place. Every male voice seemed to be his and Michelle couldn't stop her heart from racing. She found a bench to sit on so she could quiet her rumbling, painful stomach. If only the train would hurry, she thought. As if in answer to her plea, the train hissed to a stop in front of her. Stiffly, she stood. Taking a brief second to breathe she stepped aboard. She took the first empty seat and put her head down to stop the nausea. When she moved again, she placed her small suitcase under the seat. Closing her eyes she prayed for strength to reach her goal. She didn't think of what she would do when she got to Salzburg, she just knew she would be away from Max.

As the train moved out of the station, she glanced out the window, but the platform was empty. Soon she was racing away. She tried to sleep to help deal with the pain. Another spasm. She knew she was going to be sick. Hanging onto every seat for support, she made her way to the lavatory. Grateful she had taken the first available bench she did not have far to go. The door was unlocked. Shutting it she quickly fell to her knees and vomited over and over.

Michelle did not know how long she was on the floor. Finally she made herself move, though every part of her body rebelled. She sat on the little toilet and washed herself in the sink. Feeling somewhat better, she gingerly made her way back to her seat. She was alone, so she laid her head back against the window, pulled her knees to her chest to take the pressure off her stomach, and let herself drift off. She was sleeping so soundly she did not see or hear the steward as he came to check her ticket. With a shake of his head and a click of his tongue, he passed her by. The train rumbled on while she slept.

It was the hissing of the train's engine as it slowed into the station that brought Michelle out of her deep sleep. Panic seized her for a minute until she realized where she was. The pain in her belly had grown worse, but the nausea was manageable as long as she remained still. She carefully dropped her feet to the floor to tidy herself up. Immediately she regretted the movement. The pain was so searing she pulled her knees up again and took some big deep breaths. She didn't move again until the train had stopped completely in Salzburg station. She sat long enough to pull a comb through her hair while other passengers disembarked. When she did move, her knees buckled and she grabbed the seat to steady herself. After a minute she picked up the suitcase, then clutching her carry-on bag slowly made her way to the exit. As she stepped down, Michelle dropped her suitcase. Her head swam, her vision blurred. She did not hear the suitcase bounce down the steps and onto the platform. Only a moan escaped her lips as she fainted tumbling down the two stairs.

"Mrs. Enger? Michelle? Can you hear me?" Michelle could hear the voice and recognized her own name, but she couldn't find the strength to open her eyes or to even think about anything. She heard a moan and realized it had come from within herself. She was being moved and every part of her body cried out. As she was placed on a cool hard surface she groaned again and slipped back into blackness.

Sometime later Michelle surfaced. She was warm and the pain she felt was not so severe. From deep within her mind she could hear the same male voice she had heard earlier. This time, though, it sounded like she was hearing it through a tunnel. She wanted to open her eyes but struggled to do so.

"Mrs. Enger?" The man came toward her and Michelle knew she had seen him before. His voice was vaguely familiar.

"Where am I? Who are you?" She tried to pull herself up but the man restrained her with a touch of his hand on her shoulder.

"I'm Peter Zimmer, Mrs. Enger." For an instant Michelle was scared, but Peter continued before she could say anything. "I'm a doctor, Mrs. Enger, and you are in the hospital in Salzburg." Again Michelle tried to sit up. The nightmare of the past swept through her mind and she wondered if the hospital had contacted Max. Again the doctor laid her down.

"Mrs. Enger, keep still. You will only make the pain worse."

"Don't touch me!" Michelle's voice was angry. "I have to go."

"You can't leave. Your injuries are too severe. You will need several days to get better."

"I have to go," Michelle cried. "I have to...M-Max'll find me."

"Did Max do this to you? Is he your husband?"

Michelle cowered and pulled the covers tightly to her body. "I'm your doctor, Mrs. Enger. Let me help." Dr. Zimmer touched her hand white with tension as she clutched the sheet. "The ambulance brought you here and my associate, Dr. Von Brangner checked you over." Another person approached the bed. "You've taken a very bad beating. No bones are broken, but you are suffering from some abdominal bleeding and lots of bruising. Did your husband do this to you?" He waited.

Michelle hesitated and then answered his question with another one. "Does Max know I'm here? Did you call him?"

Dr. Zimmer looked up at his colleague and allowed him to answer. "No," said Dr. Von Brangner. He was facing her now. "We figured these injuries were sustained in a beating. Our examination also showed signs of possible sexual abuse. We decided to let you tell us what happened."

Michelle could feel herself redden with embarrassment. Because she was in the hospital, she knew she was not wearing her own clothes. Someone had to have undressed her, and because of her appearance she wasn't surprised that they had examined her. As she quivered under the covers at the thought, she was glad she had been sleeping when all this took place. Even though Michelle was anxious at someone touching her, the bigger feeling was one of safety. At least for the moment she did not have to be afraid.

84

Michelle closed her eyes in relief. "I don't want him to find me. I can't face him again." Her voice was no more than a whisper.

"We have given you something for the pain and we've ordered a light meal for you. As far as we know you've had nothing to eat for over twenty-four hours."

Twenty-four hours! Max must be going mad. "Oh, please don't let him find me. He'll be out looking, I know."

"You're safe here. No one is going to find you until you are ready. Now just lie back, eat a little bit, and then have a sleep. I will look in on you again later in the day." Before Peter left he gave Michelle's hand a squeeze, watched her tighten with the touch, but didn't say anything.

Max stretched his naked body under the feather tick. He groaned, rolling over as he did so. His body was stiff from lying on the floor but he felt only a slight heaviness from the liquor he had consumed. When he opened his eyes he realized he was alone. Michelle must be in the bathroom he thought, stretching his whole body languidly. He pulled himself to the bed and listened. He couldn't hear anything. Probably dressing. He strolled over to the bureau and picked up the train schedule. He read about a few of the attractions in the Innsbruck area then sat down to figure out an itinerary to the Olympic ski hill. He was beginning to feel chilled as he sat with nothing on. "What are you doing in there, Woman!" he called. "You've been in there forever."

No response or movement came from the bathroom. Only then was Max aware that something was different. He sprang to his feet. He shoved open the bathroom door only to find it empty. Panic filled him with fury. He stomped around the room to see what was gone. The torn dress and all the new things he had purchased for Michelle were sitting on the top of the bed. The closet was nearly empty. Only a few odds and ends of Michelle's still hung on hangers. One suitcase was gone...the little one. So was her purse.

Max didn't take time to shower or even clean up. He pulled on his pants and shirt and stepped outside. The air was cool so he quickly returned for a jacket. He looked at his watch. Noon. He wondered how long ago she had left. Where would she go? She had no money, no rail ticket, no passport. Oh, yes she did have her passport. He remembered. Then he thought of the Canadian money. Did she have it? He tore open the drawers, the suitcases, anything that was hers. He went through the pockets of her clothes. She wasn't that smart to hide it where he couldn't find it. Unless...Max stood seething in the middle of the room. "That devious woman!" he exclaimed out loud. "I shouldn't have let her put it away. She took that money with her." Quickly he went to his travel pouch. Yes, her rail ticket was also gone. That little witch had played him for a sucker. She must have planned this for days. She had money, her passport and her rail ticket. She could go anywhere she wanted. The rail ticket was still good for two weeks, and their airline tickets which would be picked up in Munich were dated for the same departure day so she couldn't leave Europe till then. She didn't know how to change Canadian dollars or even where to make the exchange. I'll just wait. She is so naive and stupid, she'll be back. There's no sense in me going off half-cocked. Max chuckled to himself, "She'll pay for this one. I'll show her independence and breathing space." He stepped out of his clothes and headed for the shower. At least I'll have some peace while she's gone.

When darkness fell Max was still alone. He had expected Michelle to be back long ago. It was too late tonight to try to find her, but tomorrow was another day. "You won't get away from me, you ungrateful little vixen," he called out to no one in his room. His eyes were on the expensive gifts he had purchased.

Chapter Seven

A nurse entered the room with a meal tray. Michelle realized as she smelled the broth that she was hungry. As she straightened to eat, she grabbed the side railings to steady the wave of dizziness. After a moment it subsided. "Just eat what you can," the nurse told her with a crack of a smile. "Even a little bit will make you feel better."

Michelle sipped the clear broth from the spoon. It didn't settle too well in her stomach but some of her lightheadedness went away. She finished about half of it before giving up and going back to sleep. She was resting well when the nurse came back for the tray.

The sun had fallen behind the Austrian mountains when Dr. Zimmer returned that evening. He greeted her and pulled a chair up to her bed. The discoloration on Michelle's face was dark black and blue streaked with yellow and purple. Her hair had been combed and tied back into a pony tail. If her eye hadn't been so swollen her beauty wouldn't have looked so marred. "Did you eat well?" he asked.

Michelle wondered why he looked so relaxed. What was he doing here so late at night? However, she answered his question, "I didn't do too badly, but food doesn't agree with me much yet."

"It'll probably take a few days. Dr. Von Brangner says the

internal injuries are quite nasty so that's why you don't feel like eating. Michelle," Peter Zimmer spoke cautiously. "Do you feel like telling me what happened?"

Michelle didn't want to answer. It would have been easy to slip into her little secret world, but the only image that came to her mind was Max's sprawled body on the bed. Her eyes were looking at the doctor, but he knew she was not focusing on him. "Michelle."

"Max didn't call me Michelle very often and never..."she didn't finish. She suddenly felt shy and vulnerable. She shouldn't be talking to this stranger about Max.

"I can call you Michelle, can't I?" He didn't wait for the nod. "You can call me Peter, okay?"

"But..."

"Peter is much less formal. Doctor sounds so old for some reason. You can call me Doctor when I'm doctoring. Right now I'm just your friend. Now, can you answer my question?" He didn't look much like a doctor either with his green turtle neck sweater and grey cord pants.

"Question?" Michelle was fidgety, picking at the seam on the edge of the bed sheet.

"What were you doing on the train by yourself?"

"Escaping," Michelle whispered, "Just escaping."

"Have you left Max, then?" Michelle nodded. "Is Max here in Salzburg?"

Michelle's eyes filled with panic. "I h-hope not."

"Where did you leave him?"

It took Michelle a few minutes to remember the city. "Innsbruck," she stated simply.

"Tell me why you came to Salzburg?" Michelle wiped a hand over her swollen mouth. She was so dry. Peter handed her a drink of water from her night table and waited for her to answer. She took a few sips and handed the glass back to him.

"What made you come to Salzburg?" he asked again once she lay back on her pillow.

"I-I just needed a place to go...and that was the only place I could think of." Michelle's eyelids dropped. "I was s-so scared."

Peter leaned forward, placing his hand on the covers. Michelle watched the movement but didn't raise her eyes. Peter went on. "I'm glad you didn't go any further. The internal bleeding would have gotten much worse. Besides," he added making the atmosphere a little lighter, "I'm here."

This time Michelle raised her brown eyes. "But why did it have to be you? Is it a coincidence you are always turning up?"

"Oh, you remember me, then?" His smile put deep grooves around his eyes and Michelle was reminded of their last meeting.

"I remember you in Interlaken, but even then I thought you had a familiar face." She yawned unexpectedly.

Peter rose from his chair. "Think back to Neptune and his spear," he said placing the chair against the wall again, "the Pitti Palace...Florence."

"Oh yes." Michelle gave him a little protected grin.

"So whether it is coincidence or not, providence has put us together again." Michelle knew Peter was about to leave, but he said as he leaned closer to her, "Look Michelle, I'm doing some research at various hospitals in Europe, even to taking on some of the shifts. That's why I was in emergency when the call came in about you. Sometimes I can arrange my working days to do some touring while I'm here. That's why we keep bumping into each other. I'm not on shift again until Monday and so I'm not going to let you out of my sight until I know you are safe and well. Now, I have to meet with a fellow colleague, but I'll be back in the morning. The medication Dr.

Von Brangner gave you will ensure that you have a good night's sleep. I'll see you in the morning."

Michelle felt like a vulnerable little girl. Her bottom lip quivered. "Are you sure Max won't find me here?"

Peter returned to the side of her bed. He wanted to take hold of her hand to reassure her, but knew better.

"No, Michelle, I will not let him find you. I am glad you are away from him. No person has the right to strike another, especially a spouse. Now put everything out of your mind and go to sleep." He patted the bed and walked away.

"Thank you," Michelle whispered. She knew she was safe.

Michelle was sleeping soundly when Peter returned three hours later. The nurse was just going in with the medicine tray. "Leave her medication with me. If she wakes up I'll give it to her. Right now she's sleeping and I don't want to wake her."

"There's no need for you to stay, Doctor. We'll watch her."

"Under the circumstances, nurse. I'd like to keep an eye on her. We wouldn't want any intruders."

"I understand," she said handing Peter the medication. He quietly walked over to Michelle's bed. The bruises stood out even in the darkness. He gently lifted her wrist to take her pulse and hoped she wouldn't stir. Satisfied with the results he settled himself into the lounge chair sitting in the corner.

When Michelle awoke the next morning she realized there was someone else in the room. She could hear his breathing. A man's breathing. Immediately she panicked and her heart began to race. She gulped in mouthfuls of air as she slowly opened her eyes. She wondered if she had imagined the noise. It hadn't been very loud and she didn't hear it now. Just as she was about to reprimand herself for being so paranoid, a man cleared his throat. Michelle jerked to a sitting position. She gasped, afraid to turn. Peter hurried to her bedside. "It's me," he said running his fingers through his unruly curls. "Don't worry."

"What are you doing here?" She stopped to catch her breath. "I thought you had gone."

"I did go, but I told you I'd be back. I brought you another sleeping pill in case you woke up."

"I don't recall waking up. In fact, I feel quite rested and very hungry."

"You should be," Peter said looking at his watch. "Breakfast will be here in twenty minutes."

"So I actually slept throughout the night."

"Probably the medication you were given. You know," he said coming around the bed to stand closer, "other than a face full of rainbow colors you appear much better this morning."

"I must be a mess," Michelle said brushing the loose hair out of her face.

"The colors will go away in a few days. Tell you what. I'm going to go freshen up. I'll send a nurse to help you shower. Then we'll chat over breakfast."

"I don't need a nurse," Michelle said as she slid off the bed. Peter caught her when her legs threatened to dump her on the floor.

"She'll make sure you have stable legs. Your body has had one big trauma, let's not add to it." Peter went to the door. "I'll be back as soon as you're dressed." He left with a big smile.

Michelle stood for a moment, making sure her legs would hold her up. "Good morning, Mrs. Enger. Dr. Zimmer says you'd like a shower. Here are some clean clothes." With that the nurse stayed until Michelle had showered and dressed. She did all right in the shower but was glad the nurse was able to help her with her clothes. She couldn't believe how fast she got tired, how much she still hurt, and how black her tummy was. She wondered if she would ever know how she got those bruises. They were almost as colorful as those on her face. She had to look twice when she saw her reflection in the mirror. She really was a mess.

When Peter knocked and entered, Michelle was sitting in a chair looking at the purplish mountains against the blue sky. "Pretty impressive for this time of year, isn't it?" he asked.

"Is it?"

"It's October. We could have five feet of snow. This fall has been exceptionally warm." He was by her table now and didn't make any remarks about her appearance. "I've ordered enough breakfast to feed an army. It will be here shortly." Before he could sit in the chair he had just pulled up to the little table, the door burst open and two trays were set before them. Peter uncovered the trays as soon as the staff left. "Eat up," he said as he poured her a coffee.

Once she had eaten all she could Peter took the trays and set them on the night trolley. He had left Michelle sipping a second cup of coffee. "So," he said, "have you thought about what you would like to do? It won't be too long before Dr. Von Brangner discharges you."

Michelle set the coffee cup down. "I don't usually do the thinking. Max makes the decisions..." She dropped her head shamefully.

"You made some decisions recently. You left Innsbruck on your own and made it this far."

She looked at him directly as if to remind him of her circumstances. "Only out of desperation."

"If you hadn't been so sick, I'm sure you would have figured it out."

"Had I not been so sick, I probably wouldn't have left. That's the rea..." She couldn't finish.

"It doesn't matter. You're away from Max, so let's consider

your options." He placed his hand briefly over Michelle's cupped ones, then quickly removed them. She needed to feel the touch but he didn't want to frighten her. She passed him a fleeting troubled look but relaxed when his hand lifted. Peter continued as if the interchange had not happened. "You are in a foreign country. That will govern some of your plans, but most important is the question, are you going back to your husband?"

Myriads of questions went through Michelle's mind. Should she break up her family? What would the children think? How could she earn a living? Where would she go? Maybe Max wouldn't be angry. Maybe he didn't mean to hurt her.

Michelle's memory went back to the morning she left and the night before. The pain had been so bad she couldn't even escape into her fantasy world. She remembered the hair pulling, the vulgar names, the harsh rough hands, and her tears. But the more she cried the more times he hit her. She recalled reaching out of the darkness and crying, but a blow to her belly threw her back into oblivion. "What choice do I have?" she finally said.

"You always have a choice and you've already made a start. In fact, you've done the hard part. You left." He gave her a reassuring smile.

"I couldn't do it again," she told him.

"You don't have to. You've done it now." He stopped to let that sink in. "Let me tell you something from my experience as a doctor. Once a spouse uses physical force to accomplish his desires, he will always do it. Sometimes with help he can get over it, but it takes a long time and an entire change in personality."

"I couldn't face Max again right now. I can't even imagine being around him. I think I'd die first."

"Then that's step number two, at least for now. So what about going home?"

"I'm afraid Max would be there, or that he would come there." Her voice was a whimper. "I figure that's the first place he'd look."

"What were your holiday plans? When were you scheduled to go home?"

"We were to go on Sunday November sixth."

"That's about two weeks from now." Peter stopped. He had to give her some idea of what she could do. "Were your tickets open or was the sixth the earliest you could leave?" Before Michelle could answer, Peter had another thought. "Do you have your ticket, Michelle? We could phone and check it out."

Michelle went to her purse to look but knew she hadn't thought of her ticket. Taking out her passport and the rail pass she said, "Max didn't even want me carrying my own passport but the border officials told him I should carry it myself in case we got separated." She gave a little laugh. "What would they think of their advice now?" She returned to the table. "I don't have the ticket, but I have these." She handed them to Peter. He set them on the table.

"What is your money situation like? Do you have any?"

Michelle, who was standing, blushed, feeling a little guilty. "I took Max's Austrian money off the bureau when I left. Oh, he'll be mad."

"How much was it?'

"I had it in the pants pocket I was wearing." She looked around the room to find them.

"They're on the shelf in the closet," Peter told her. "I'll get them." Michelle walked with him but it was Peter who took them down and searched the pockets. He dumped the money on the table. "Not quite thirty schillings," he stated after counting it. "It's not going to get you very far but it will keep you eating for a day or two. What about a credit card? I don't suppose you have one?" Michelle was shaking her head even before Peter had finished answering the question. "Well, that could limit your poss...."

"Oh," Michelle exclaimed. "I forgot Max's stash." Hurriedly she went to her small suitcase in the closet. Peter took it from her and put it on the bed. Michelle took a second for the pain in her stomach to subside, then she opened the case. She picked out the sewing kit and slowly opened it. She drew out the folded bills and handed them to Peter. "Max liked cash. It made him feel important when he could wave it around."

"How did you come by it?" Peter followed Michelle back to the little table where she wearily sat down.

"He had me keep half our money when he misplaced his wallet. He thought he had lost it all so he had me put some away."

"So," Peter stated, "that takes care of another hurdle. You have the money to do what you want. You just need to decide about going home. Staying in a foreign country for very long is probably not wise."

"I miss my children. I want to be closer to them. But I don't know about going home..."

"What about your children? Could you stay with them?" Peter was aware of Michelle's fatigue but wanted to cover some of the options with her before he let her rest.

"Anna and Sonja live near a university campus where they attend classes. Our son Billy is a chef in Montreal."

"Could you stay with them?" he repeated.

"The girls don't have room. Besides, that would be the first place Max would look. He knows how close I am to them."

"And your son?"

She sighed. "He might be a possibility, at least for a little while.

"Good. Then a phone call to him would answer any questions you have there. When you are well, we will phone the airlines and see about your ticket, or purchasing another, and then we will phone your kids. I think the best thing for you is to be with your family. Come on," he motioned to the bed. "Have a rest. I'm going to go pester a professor about a medical thesis I think he scored too low. I won't be gone long." Michelle climbed back onto the bed. A look of anxiety met Peter as he turned to say good-bye. "I've got people watching your room. No one will be let in without my permission." Michelle lay down. Her mind was full but she was too tired to think. It didn't take her long to fall asleep.

Thinking that Michelle was somewhere close, Max packed his suitcases but left them in the Pension Aberbrun. He clipped his money pouch around his waist, picked up the train schedule, and left the room. He stood on the street not quite sure where to start. If I were Michelle, where would I go? Max asked himself. She'd need to feel safe, so maybe a hostel of some kind. Lots of tourists stayed in hostels, they were cheaper. But money wouldn't be a factor, he thought, if she found a way to cash in some of the Canadian currency. No, the hostel was the most likely place. Max leaned on a post while he thumbed through the train book. It was a good thing they put hotels and such in it. It took him more time than he expected to find the listings, so when he figured out a travel plan to cover each one as quickly as he could, he had missed the train and had to wait. His impatience showed as he flipped the book open and closed. He chewed on his nails and twisted his mustache. By the time he had boarded the train he was so angry at Michelle for spoiling the holiday, he was pale. His anger made him make mistakes and he missed the stop for the first hostel so he had to backtrack. By nightfall of the second night that Michelle had been gone, he had been to as many hostels as he could find advertised plus a couple of new ones that had just opened. He had only taken enough time out to grab a coffee and scone so he was ravenous when he returned to the hotel. Flopping down on one of the beds, he was so irate he couldn't even think what he would like to eat. He still had most of the two thousand dollars left that he was carrying, and he still had his credit card. What he didn't have was his wife.

He sat for a while, then decided to go to the nearest pub for a meal and several drinks. The liquor acted like a sleeping pill and he slept like a dead man. As he dressed the next morning, he seethed at himself in the mirror for sleeping in so long. Now, he would have to go faster. Today he would search the local hotels and if he didn't have success there he would phone home to the girls and then go to the police. Grabbing a coffee before leaving the pension, he gulped it down and left. He had a lot of hotels to cover and wanted to visit each one himself and not just call them on the phone. Michelle might have bribed them not to tell him she was there. It would be a long day.

Chapter Eight

Michelle didn't know if her nervousness and agitation were from fear or excitement. Dr. Von Brangner had pronounced her well enough to be discharged and she hovered near the window wondering what to do. She had become quite attached to the hospital room and its security, though the mountains and sunshine outside were very inviting. Being in the hospital for these five days had given her time to heal. Her appetite had returned and she went for long walks in the corridors. Her physical self was healing, but her emotions weren't. She tensed when people passed by her or when the nurse took her vital signs. She knew it was unnatural, but there didn't seem to be anything she could do about it.

Dressed in her own clothes now, Michelle decided to leave. Peter had stopped by after his Monday morning meeting and told her he would be back just after lunch to take her out. Michelle didn't even hear him when he entered the room. "I see you are all packed." His face was lit up; his voice sounded pleased. Michelle's suitcase, carry-on bag, purse and jacket were lying on the bed.

"It looks lovely outside," Michelle said, not knowing what else to say. She couldn't even bring herself to turn to face the doctor for fear he would see her agitation.

"It's a bit cool but a lovely day to be outside." He was

beside her now. "There's more and more snow in the mountains every day. It's into the trees now."

"I've been watching it," Michelle told him. "I can't wait to be outside to smell the crisp clean air."

"So what are we waiting for. On with your jacket." Michelle let him pick up her coat off the bed and bring it to her. Her feet were heavy and she couldn't bring herself to move. "You'll love being outdoors."

"B-b-but..."

"We'll go to the foyer and make some calls. I will call the airlines, you call your children. We'll start there," he reassured her knowing she probably didn't know where to begin. Peter carried her suitcase and set it down near the phone booths. "You call your girls just to make sure they're fine. I wouldn't tell them right now where you are just in case Max talks to them. I'm going to call Air Canada to check on the tickets."

"Air Canada?" Michelle questioned, not moving.

"Your baggage tag says Air Canada, so I'll start there."

"Oh," Michelle felt silly.

"Now, call your Anna. You'll want to hear her voice."

Michelle stepped into the booth but left the door open. The operator put her through right away. Both girls should still be up, it was only 9:30 p.m. in Toronto. Sonja, picked up the phone on the second ring. "Hello." Michelle couldn't speak. "Hello?" came Sonja's voice again. On the third hello Michelle finally found her tongue.

"Hello," came the hoarse whisper.

"Mom? Mom? Is that you? Where are you? I can hardly hear you!"

Michelle straightened as if doing so would give her voice more volume. "I'm here."

Sonja rushed on..."We've been so worried. Dad called yesterday. He wanted to know if we had heard from you or if you had come home. What's going on Mom?" There was a banging and clatter on the line.

"Mom!" It was Anna now. "Are you okay? We were so worried about you?"

Michelle could hardly stand to hear the concern in the girls' voices. The tears from her eyes were running down her cheeks. "Oh, Anna, Sonja."

"I'm on the extension in the bedroom, Mom," she heard Sonja say. "Now please tell us what's going on. We have been terribly worried since you called the last time."

Michelle couldn't stop the feelings of guilt, but somewhere she got the strength and courage to speak. "I'm okay for now. I just wanted to hear your voices and let you know I'll be home soon."

"What are you trying to tell us, Mom?" Sonja was her objective self now. "Where's Dad? He sounded furious when he called."

Michelle wasn't sure how much to tell them at the moment. She didn't even know if she could, but she felt she had to tell them something. "I-I've left your father." She paused. "But I'm okay."

"Is that why he phoned here? Yes, that explains his questions." said Sonja.

"What did he say?" asked Michelle her eyes darting around the room as if Max were going to interrupt this call. Instead she focused on Peter who was still talking in the other booth.

"Dad wanted to know if you had called. I figured he was just checking up on you like he usually does. I told Anna that your conversation from Switzerland had not been cut off, that it was probably Dad who disconnected the line. However, since we didn't know anything when he phoned we had nothing to tell him. It made him furious. He even asked if you were here.

That really got me thinking."

Anna was sniffling. "So where are you, Mom?"

"I-I'd better not tell you in case your father phones you again. I don't want you to have to lie to him, but I am feeling better and will try to get back to Canada as soon as I can."

"W-Were you sick, Mom?" Anna asked and Michelle scolded herself for not watching what she said. However, Sonja didn't give her time to explain.

"Did he hit you again, Mom? Was that why you left?" Sonja sounded angry.

"I'm doing okay and will try to keep in touch with you. As soon as I know my plans I'll tell you but for now I can't deal with your father knowing where I am."

"We won't even tell him we talked to you if he phones again."

"No," Michelle told them. "He knows me. He knows I couldn't go very long without speaking to you. Just tell him I called but you don't know where I am. He may not believe you but you can't tell him what you don't know." Michelle felt better knowing that her girls now knew what was going on.

"Can you at least tell us if you're alone?" Sonja asked. "Do I need to come to you?"

"The doctor is here..." Again she could have bit her tongue.

"A doctor?" Sonja explained. "Did you have to go to the hospital?"

"I can't tell you any more, girls. Just know I'm fine and getting some plans together. It is imperative, though, that you say nothing to your Dad. You don't know where I am and that is all he needs to know." Michelle couldn't believe how brave she sounded when her soul was filled with fear. Not just for herself but for her family, and even some for Max. He must be going out of his mind. "I'm going to call Billy now. He needs to hear from me as well. I'll keep in touch." Michelle didn't tell the girls about her needing to stay with Billy. She didn't want them to know of her plans for fear Max would get to Billy first. After saying good-bye she got the operator to connect her with her son in Montreal. Max had not phoned Billy yet so he knew nothing of her circumstances. Michelle talked more openly to him but didn't fill him in on the details. Billy didn't think his father would check with him, but he assured Michelle he would keep their conversation confidential. He had no qualms about lying to his father even though she didn't want him to. "You don't have to tell me about my father, Mom. I wish he could be different, then maybe I could feel differently about him. No, you come when you can. I've got room. Just don't let him talk you into going back. You should have left him long ago. I'm glad you have help. Good luck."

Peter was standing outside the booth watching the people come into the hospital when Michelle hung up the phone. She too was glad she had help. He turned when he heard the door of the phone booth close. He could tell by her pale but more calm appearance that the conversations had been favorable. He immediately began to tell her about the airlines. "You and Max were scheduled to leave Frankfurt on November sixth, though they are not confirmed seats. There's no way of telling whether Max has inquired about you. He may figure you might try to cash in the reservation which is in the computer and go early. Or, if he realizes you have his money, he may think you purchased your own ticket. I don't think though..."

"No," Michelle said a little apologetically. "Max doesn't think I know how to do anything. He has checked with the girls and was surprised that I hadn't talked to them...if he believes them. No, he has probably checked with the airlines, called the police, and checked all the train stations in Innsbruck. If the agent remembers me, Max could be very close on my trail by now. It's been five days.

Max, though, had not given Michelle credit on using the train. It was the morning of Michelle's discharge before he even decided to check with the train station. It had taken him two days to go to all the hotels in Innsbruck and the smaller surrounding communities. He didn't even phone the girls until the fourth day. He didn't want to believe that Michelle hadn't talked to them, but he knew they wouldn't lie to him. Michelle hadn't called and she wasn't there so she still must be around Innsbruck somewhere. "Oh damn," he said outloud as he dressed on the morning of the fifth day. "Why didn't I think about this before? I bet that little dreamer went back to Switzerland. She would do something like that because she had been there before. She liked her 'breathing space' there." He drawled out the words sarcastically. Now that he was sure where to find her, he hurried.

It was at the train station that he decided to make inquiries. In his anger he had not thought to do this before. He figured Michelle didn't have the brains to do anything on her own but somehow she had found a way to leave Innsbruck. She must be back in Switzerland. The agent at the station did not remember Michelle. Had he been on duty that early morning, he would have remembered the bruised and battered woman struggling to get her suitcase onto the train. It was fortunate for her it had been his day off. He didn't think to mention this to Max. Max boarded the train and it sped off, back toward Frau Schmidt's in Interlaken.

Peter picked up Michelle's suitcase. "Well, where shall we go now?"

Michelle didn't have a clue. "Anywhere," she told him. "Some place I can sit and think. I can't stay here, I know Max is getting closer to me."

Peter stepped outside holding the door open for her. "Taxi!" he called. Michelle allowed him to help her inside and then he placed her suitcase in the trunk. "Mirabellgarten," he said to the driver.

"Where are we going?" asked Michelle.

"Some place where Max cannot find you should he come to Salzburg. Some place where you can rest and think. You can't get over-tired, but you have to make some decisions, and I don't want Max finding you before you're ready."

"I wish I wasn't so afraid," Michelle told him, her hands twitching the strap of her purse. Peter wanted to hold her, to quiet her fears, but didn't feel he had the right.

"Are you that afraid of Max?" he asked and wanted to strike out at the man who had hurt this beautiful woman.

"Of M-Max...and my decision to leave him."

"Are you doubting your decision?

"Some. I have as many fears being away as I did when I was with him. Maybe more."

"Could you see yourself going through another beating? You'll always have that to face, if you go back."

Michelle watched the marble and stone buildings as they passed by. "I guess I'm scared of being alone. I don't know how I will live. I don't know what I should do."

Peter placed his hand over hers. She stiffened with a gasp, but he gave her hand a gentle squeeze and held it tenderly. "I will do all I can to help," he said close to her ear, "not hurt." He sat back but did not release her hand. He needed to comfort her as much as he knew she needed the comfort even though she might find his touch disturbing. "You don't have anything to fear from me. I only want what's best for you."

Michelle wanted to cry, her tight chest bursting. "Part of me knows that. The other part just wants to run. I can't imagine anyone taking time for me. I don't know why anyone, especially you, would want to do this. You must have a reason?" Michelle's gaze did not leave the window though she was not aware of the people on the sidewalks, of the mountains in the background, or the lush green that filled every empty spot. All she could deal with at this moment was to try to understand the tenderness of Peter's hands and the softness of his voice. It was unusual and she didn't know how to read his intentions.

"Not every man has ulterior motives for doing something. Sometimes we do it just because we care." Peter now lifted his hand from hers. The relief showed in her face. It's a start, though, he thought. "You know Michelle, I have an intense dislike for people who get their jollies by abusing others. I have to admire you for having the courage to leave after so many years, and in a strange place. I can't help but feel you need someone to help, and I would appreciate being that person." He waited for her to take this in. "That is the only motive I have."

"I guess I'm just afraid?" She gave him a brief look.

"I would be too; I won't do anything to harm you. I am not a big bad wolf stalking a little crippled animal. My goal is to get you safely home."

"I don't know what I would do without you."

"It's supposed to be this way. I'm one who believes that everything happens for a purpose. You were supposed to come into my life. Will you trust me now?"

Michelle knew she didn't have any choice, so she only nodded. The taxi slowed to a stop along a hedge-lined curb. Once on the sidewalk Peter paid the driver while speaking to him in fluent German. He turned to Michelle as the taxi drove off. "I told the driver to come back in an hour. He'll care for your suitcase and pack so we don't have to carry it around."

"My money?" Michelle watched the car drive away.

"It's safe. He'll just go for a coffee while he waits. I paid him a generous tip."

Peter led Michelle through an opening in the thick squarely trimmed hedge. She stopped just inside. Sitting on a hill was the largest white marble mansion she had ever seen. All around it were immaculate gardens of flowers and shrubs. Numerous oversized statues standing on large pedestals formed a cavalcade around the perimeter. A magnificent fountain in the center sprayed water high into the air. The sun's rays topped it with a clear and full rainbow.

"It's breathtaking isn't it?" Peter asked but it was more a statement. "I never tire of its beauty."

Michelle was already taking photographic memories to file away. "What is this place?" In slow motion she panned the area from where she stood.

"This is Mirabellgarten. Yonder is The Castle. The ancient archbishops who once lived here loved beauty, history and art. All the statues you see here are Roman and Greek, ranging from Apollo to David." He took her by the hand and she trembled. "Let's find an empty bench in the sunshine. You must be tired."

Michelle and Peter sat on the nearest bench, the sun warm on their backs. Michelle was close enough to the fountain to see the layer of coins on the bottom of the water. It was clear with a variety of fish floating aimlessly about. "This is wonderful. I could stay here forever."

Peter let her relax and enjoy the surroundings. After a few minutes he asked, "Feeling better?"

"Yes," said Michelle.

Peter smiled warmly at her. "Do you feel like talking?'

"I don't want to, but I know I should." Michelle dropped her head. "Billy says I can stay with him. He suggested I fly right into Montreal and he will pick me up."

"Is that what you've decided to do then?" Peter was

pleased she had been doing some planning.

"My preference would be to stay with the girls, but I think staying with Billy until I figure out what I am going to do in the future is my best plan. I can go to the girls then."

"Good. Doesn't it feel a little less frightening knowing you have made that decision and that you have a safe place to go?" His smile was so reassuring Michelle felt herself quiver. He really does care, she thought. Peter turned on the seat to face Michelle. "I agree that you need to get back to Canada as soon as you can. As long as you stay here there is a greater chance Max will find you. When I talked to Air Canada they said you needed your ticket to return on the same flight plan, whether you change days or not. So it looks like you will have to purchase a new ticket on another flight to make it harder for Max to trail you!"

"I have the money, don't I?" Michelle didn't feel any panic about that.

"Oh yes, and plenty to live on once you return home. At least for a while. Now, some of the calls I made were to other airlines. You want to go quickly so that will limit your possibilities. However, there are some European airlines that can fly directly to Toronto and probably Montreal that will get you out of here in a couple of days. The best one I found was Lufthansa Air out of Munich.

Michelle cried out. "I couldn't do that!"

"Why?"

"I-I-I can't speak German. It would be so foreign. Max was the one who knew the language."

Peter chuckled and touched Michelle's arm reassuringly. "No, Michelle. You'd enjoy it. They speak English quite well. I travel Lufthansa all the time. They're very friendly. Let's hope Max will think you are traveling with a Canadian airlines out of Frankfurt, so we'll send you home on a nonstop flight on a

German line from a different city. It only makes sense."

Michelle thought for a moment. It did seem logical, but could she do it alone? Suddenly her mind went back to the flight over to Europe and the contrast between the beauty outside the window, the emotion of Anna's music, and Max's sternness beside her. The more she thought about it, the more appealing it became. "Maybe I can do it," she stated aloud.

"Good," Peter said lifting her by her hand. "When we get near a phone I'll make the arrangements for you. I'll even take you to Munich myself. Now, let's forget all this for the time being and let me show you around. We have half an hour before the taxi comes back."

Michelle lost herself in the history and culture as Peter told about each statue. By the time they were back at the entrance waiting for their taxi, Michelle felt as though she knew every character individually. They made a short stop at an enormous sized church where they enjoyed the domes, the turrets, the spires and stained glass windows. Peter walked reverently ahead of her opening the heavy mahogany doors. They didn't speak; they absorbed the spirit of the building.

Once back in the taxi Peter told Michelle to lay her head back and relax. He was going to take her to a local hotel where he would find her a room and make the call to the airlines. Then they would find a place to have some dinner. Michelle was so weary, she welcomed the chance to lean back and close her eyes.

"Michelle?" The voice penetrated Michelle's subconscious and she jerked awake. "Hey, it's okay!" exclaimed Peter. "We're at the hotel." The taxi was pulling into the covered courtyard. Michelle, so tired her body ached, just wanted to lie down. Peter stepped out of the taxi and extended a hand to Michelle. Even her knees felt wobbly. "It's been a big day for you. Maybe we'll just order a meal in." He carried her bags into the building and stopped at the desk. After a few words to the desk clerk he took the key and gave it to Michelle. "This is your room until we go to Munich," he told her. "It has a nice view of the hospital where I work, and the Salzburg Monastery is on the side of the mountain behind it."

"But..." Michelle held the key tightly.

"I've put the registration on my credit card, but tomorrow we'll get your money out so you can do some of these things yourself. You might as well start right now becoming more independent. Okay?" The warmth of his smile reassured her.

Michelle's room was on the fifth floor, not too high up to make her nervous but high enough to provide a wide panoramic view of the mountains and valley. Peter set the suitcase and carry bag on the dressing table. "Will you be all right while I go to my room to check my messages?" Before Michelle could answer he added, "I have a suite on the seventh floor. I always stay here because it's close to the hospital." Going to the phone he pointed to the little pad and pencil beside it. "I will leave the extension number to my room so you can call if you need me. Now enjoy the view. I'll make the airline calls from my room and hurry back so we can eat."

Michelle felt like a dummy. She didn't know what to say. Although Peter was taking a lot of the decision making from her she did not feel in any way controlled by his actions. There was a big difference between Max's control and Peter's suggestions. "Will you manage until I return?" Peter asked opening the door.

"I think so," she answered.

"Good. I won't be long." With that he shut the door behind him. Michelle dropped her purse onto the dresser beside the suitcase and stared out the window. The castle, the mountains, the streets trimmed with flower baskets and manicured shrubs were lovely to look at. She took off her coat and surveyed the room that was to be hers for tonight, anyway. The bed was queen size with a dark blue spread. The picture on the wall was a closeup of the entrance of the Salzburg Monastery, and two ancient looking Monks were sitting on a bench next to a wrought iron gate. Michelle gazed at the detail of the picture for a long time. She hoped to go there some day. If only Max... Max! Was he close by? Would he find her here? She went back to the window. Being up five stories wasn't so far that she couldn't make out the people's faces as they walked by the hotel. If Max was around and looked up, he could probably see her. She stepped away, her heart pounding at the thought. Why would he come here? I never told him I wanted to come to Salzburg. It was only an inner wish that didn't get expressed. She went back to the window. I'm not going to let my fears ruin this brief time. Unzipping her case, she took out her makeup kit and went to the bathroom to tidy herself. She was standing at the window again feeling a whole lot better when Peter knocked on her door. Michelle opened it not thinking it would be anyone else.

Chapter Nine

Peter entered Michelle's room, "Well, I've found you a way home." In his hand he held out a piece of paper he had written on. "Today is Wednesday and there is a seat in economy Saturday afternoon at four-fifty. Flight 541 out of Munich non stop to Montreal." Peter was excited. "We can go to the travel agent tomorrow to purchase your ticket now that you are registered in the computer." He was at the window with her now. "I hope Max is so far off track he won't figure out what you have done."

"What you have done," Michelle reminded him.

"No, what you have done. You made the decision and I just took it one step further. Tomorrow you will pay for your ticket and keep it with you until your flight. I really do think you will be okay. I just hope we can keep ahead of Max."

"I do too," Michelle said, "I don't know how strong I would be if he found me."

"Do you really think he could browbeat you into going back to him? Think about it now. Should he turn up somewhere out of the blue, will you be prepared?"

Michelle gave a big sigh and searched the impending darkness outside her window. Peter closed the blinds while she thought about his question. "What do you think I should do? How do I prepare myself to be strong?"

Peter carefully laid his hands on her shoulders and then lifted her chin. "You are strong, Michelle." She quivered under his touch and he dropped his hands but his gentle and sincere expression kept her attention on what he was saying. "You need to think about what you would say and what you would do should he return unexpectedly. That way it won't be so frightening. You will have made your decision already." He waited for a minute before saying, "You have the ability to make right decisions. You're safe, and I know you will reason things out."

Michelle did feel safer right now. She would pay for her ticket home tomorrow. She had a place to go and some money to do it with. The little voice inside told her Peter's words made sense. "I think I can do this," she finally whispered.

"Good. Now do you want to eat in or do you want to go out? There are eating places up and down the street and even one here in the hotel."

"I'm almost too tired to eat. Maybe we can just eat here where I don't have to use so much energy and," she paused, "where I am not so visible to the public and," she added, running her palm over her bruised cheek, "out of Max's view."

"Probably wise," Peter said. "The room service menu is under the phone. Let's order."

Max reached Interlaken just after lunch time. He scurried up to the pension and found Frau Schmidt at the front desk. She remembered him and Michelle, and asked him where she was. "Are you wanting a room?" she asked. "Where is your pretty wife?"

Max glowered at her, already knowing the answer before he asked the question, "You haven't seen my wife?"

Frau Schmidt was surprised. "No, No, Des Herrn, not since you checked out last week. Was she to return to Interl'kn?"

"I thought she might have," Max said, suddenly feeling

weary. If she wasn't here, where was she? Where else should he look? He turned away from the concerned look on Frau Schmidt's face. She would also like to know where the little wife was.

Max stood in the sunshine, not feeling its warmth. There was a train at nine tonight going back to Innsbruck. He wondered if he should take it and start all over again. Maybe, he reconsidered, Michelle might have gone to Grindlewald. Once she had come this far she might have decided to go further up where she could walk in her trees and listen to the cowbells. That was a definite possibility. He smacked his leg with his arm. Once again he felt in control. As he hurried to the train station he became more and more excited. She would soon be his again. He'd even stay with her wherever she was. He looked around him. It might even be nice to be back in this setting again. Max could only think of Michelle's body naked under a fluffy feather tick. It made him hurry all the more.

Peter and Michelle ordered a meal of boiled potatoes and schnitzel. It came smothered in large fresh mushrooms cooked to perfection, a salad, and creamy custard for dessert. After eating, Michelle felt a lot better. Watching her waist line had never been a problem. Her figure remained trim and tiny, just like Max wanted it.

"What are you thinking," Peter asked setting down his dessert spoon. "You slipped away again."

"I didn't mean to," Michelle blushed.

"You don't need to apologize. I'm sure those little reprieves are quite refreshing for you."

"And a life saver," Michelle added.

"So were you running away from something again?" His eyes wrinkled again, his smile soft.

"Not really, I was just thinking how nice it is not to have

to worry about what food I should eat. Max liked the way I look."

"I do too. You are a very lovely woman." Michelle sucked in a breath. What was he getting at? For an instant she panicked and pushed back her chair. Peter jumped up to comfort her but Michelle let out a cry. "Michelle!" Peter was beside her but did not touch her. "Michelle," he said more softly, "I didn't mean to frighten you. Haven't you ever been told how lovely you are? Look in the mirror." Something struck him then. Words that Dr. Von Brangner had said when he was examining Michelle, *There looks to be some sexual abuse here too.*

"Ooh," he took a step backwards giving her some space. "I didn't mean anything suggestive in what I said. I didn't mean to frighten you. Remember I told you I would never hurt you in any way? I mean it. You have nothing to fear from me." He watched the terror leave Michelle's eyes but something wary stayed in its place. Peter knew it would be quite a while before she fully trusted anyone again. Knowing that Dr. Brangner's diagnosis was correct angered Peter. This lady has been abused not only physically and verbally, but sexually. How much does a woman have to take? Peter turned away for fear she would see the anger on his face.

It took some time for the tension to leave the room. Peter stacked the dishes and placed the tidy tray outside the door for pickup. It was getting late but he had to ask her opinion about the next two day's plans. If she was going to be here until Saturday, he wanted to show her some of the sights. Again he hoped Max was so involved somewhere else he wouldn't think of coming to the places Peter figured Michelle would like. When he thought she had gotten over the trauma he asked, "What would you like to do on Thursday and Friday once we purchase your airline ticket from the travel agent?"

Michelle didn't answer for a time, then she took a deep

breath and answered softly, almost afraid to make a suggestion. "I-I'd sure like to see the Salzburg Castle. I've always wanted to see where Julie Andrews played Maria. Other than that I don't know of anything else to go see."

Peter kept his distance. "Will you let me be your guide? It would be fun to go to the castle with someone who would appreciate the setting. We might even get to climb the hill at the back of the monastery so you can run and sing in the hills."

Michelle didn't know what to say. She could only imagine herself singing. "I would like that," she said simply.

"I'm going to run to the hospital for a few minutes, but I won't be half an hour. I want to make sure I won't be on any schedules until after the weekend. I want to spend this time with you. Do you think you can get ready for bed and spend the night by yourself? I could call back later."

"I'll be fine, I think. I don't believe Max can find me here."

"Lock your door and deadbolt it when I leave. I will tell the desk clerk you are a patient and that you are not to be disturbed under any circumstances. I will phone you when I return from the hospital. Think you can manage?"

Michelle nodded her head. "I will just go to bed."

"I'll come get you for breakfast about eight. We can go to the travel agent and catch the eleven o'clock tour to the monastery and castle."

Peter left. Michelle heard him walk away as soon as she had slid the deadbolt in place. By the time he phoned she was in her nightgown, her walkman on her ears and resting to the music of Placido Domingo. "Good night, Michelle," he said over the phone. "Sweet dreams."

"Thank you, Peter," she said.

Peter couldn't help admiring the woman just two floors

down. He had been drawn to her when he saw her with Neptune in Florence. It took all his courage not to snatch her off the trail in Grindlewald, and if he had known then what he did now about Max, he might have done that. No one should have to suffer brutality. It was with those thoughts and the excitement he felt about the next two and a half days that he went to bed. He only hoped and prayed Michelle would have a good night and trust him until he could see her safely on her way home.

Salzburg Castle, the monk monastery, and the rolling hills held the magic for Michelle she knew it would. Their tour guide showed them the mansion, the little white gazebo in the garden where Maria had been kissed by Captain Von Trapp, and the river where Maria had fallen from the boat with the Von Trapp children. She stood in awe in the great chapel in the cathedral where Maria and the Captain were married. Her most favorite spot however was the meadow. "This is called Mondsee or Moon-Lake," Peter told her. "The place where Maria sang and ran free in the breeze." He encouraged Michelle to sit on the grass. It would be a good place for her to rest so she didn't get too tired. He didn't even feel as though he was doing her a favor. The sheer enjoyment on her face was pleasure enough for him.

It was well into the afternoon when Peter and Michelle left the castle. They had lunched at a small sidewalk cafe, but ate indoors, the October breeze a bit too chilly to eat outside. They were on the bus back to the city center when Michelle asked, spelling out the word, "What is a D-a-c-h-a-u?"

Peter straightened, a scowl clouding his face. "Where did you hear that?"

"I didn't hear it. It's right there, on the poster."

Peter looked to where Michelle was pointing and saw the advertisement. "That is Dachau," he enunciated clearly.

"Oh, I heard Max talk about that place. He told me it was

a place we needed to visit because it would be an educational experience for me."

Peter's disgust showed on his face. "I'm not surprised he'd say that. Dachau is a German concentration camp left over from the war. It has been turned into a memorial now, but with its placards and graphic billboards, it is a very hideous place to visit. It is a morbid display of a time in our history that is best remembered as a great tragedy. I don't think it would be a place you would enjoy visiting."

"It doesn't sound like it," Michelle said reflectively, "not after the lovely experience I've just had."

It was very late by the time they had had dinner and returned to the hotel. Salzburg was lit up and music played in every restaurant and cafe. Michelle was very tired but it was a very pleasant fatigue. Once Peter had said good night, she bolted the door and prepared for bed. As she lay under the warm quilt, with Julie Andrews singing, "The Hills Are Alive," from a tape she had purchased during the tour, Michelle realized she hadn't thought of Max most of the day. She fell asleep thinking she was living in an unbelievable dream.

Max, on the other hand, sat fuming on the nine o'clock train back to Innsbruck. No matter where he looked or walked he found no traces of Michelle. How could she have disappeared so quickly and effectively? Never once did he ever consider foul play. She simply had abandoned him. Tomorrow he would check with his girls again, and the police. He'd choose one of the photos he'd taken of Michelle during their trip and have it blown up so it could be circulated. He knew he had to hurry, there were just ten days of holiday left. Every time he thought about Michelle putting him through this he would conjure up in his mind ways she would pay. He was not one to be toyed with.

The ringing of the phone made Anna jump. Sonja was in the bathroom drying her hair so Anna answered on the second ring. "Hello."

"Anna!" Her name was said harshly and she knew it was her father. She wished Sonja had picked up the phone. "Yes," she said timidly her voice a high squeak.

Max took no notice. "Have you heard from your mother?"

Anna hesitated trying to pick her words carefully. Her mouth was so dry her tongue wouldn't fit around the words. Oh, Sonja, she pleaded inwardly, hurry, you would know what to say. "Anna!" Anna jumped at the tone of his voice. It sounded as though he was standing right beside her. "Y-yes, Daddy."

The noise of the dryer shut off in the bathroom while Max hollered. "When did she phone? Where was she calling from?" He knew Michelle couldn't go too long without talking to his girls. He would find her now.

Anna started to whimper. "S-she called y-yester—no the d-day before I think."

"Well, which was it?"

"I don't remember!" Anna cried out loud. "I-I...." Anna heard the click of the phone.

"Hi, Dad." Sonja said, as confident as usual.

"Thank goodness, I couldn't make any sense out of that child's words." Max's tone had quietened down but was still harsh. "Anna said your mother called? Was it yesterday or the day before?"

Sonja was prepared. She had been waiting for her father to call. "Mom called on Wednesday."

"Not till then?'

"No, I told you on Tuesday that she hadn't called. That was the truth."

"Where is she?" Max demanded so sharply Sonja just wanted to hang up on him, but she had rehearsed her response and knew what to say.

"She didn't give us any details and she didn't tell us where she was. What's happened Dad? How did you get separated?," she asked as innocently as she could. She wondered what he would tell her.

The question caught Max off guard and he had to think quickly. "Oh," he paused long enough to come up with an response, "your mother got some wild idea about needing breathing space. She left one morning while I was sleeping."

"Without provocation?" Sonja asked, pleased that she had thought of that question.

"That's between me and your mother. Are you sure she didn't tell you where she was? Anna? Are you still on the phone? One of you answer me." He was hollering again.

Anna whispered into the phone, "S-she said s-she was b-bet..."

"She didn't tell us anything, Dad," Sonja jumped in. He might as well hear it all. "She said she would not tell us so we wouldn't have to lie to you. She doesn't want you to find her." Max's vulgarity was more than Sonja could take and she snapped the phone back onto its cradle, cutting her father off.

Max was furious. He threw the phone onto the desk not bothering to hang it up. He stomped around the room. What was the matter with everybody? Had they lost their senses? He had to find Michelle. The girls weren't going to help. He had no wish to speak to Billy and he was sure Michelle wouldn't. They got along but had never been close. The police had to be his next option. It was midnight now. Digging through the photos he had taken since the holiday began, he found one of Michelle while in Italy. He set it on the dresser. A few hours sleep then he would take it to the police and by midmorning it would be circulating all over this area. Unless he got special permission from the authorities he knew he couldn't distribute them out of Austria. No, he would try this first. Michelle wouldn't be too far away.

The weather stayed sunny on Thursday so Peter took Michelle to other attractions in and around Salzburg. Several times through the day she would panic when she thought she saw Max in the crowd. Peter was anxious also. He took Michelle's concerns seriously. It was definitely conceivable for Max to be getting closer so he tried to take Michelle to places he didn't think Max would go like Nonnberg Abbey and Holy Trinity Church. They stopped for dinner in the roof cafe at Hotel Stein just as the sun was setting. As they walked up the steep hill Michelle's shoe caught on a cobblestone. "Ooh," she cried. Before she could fall, Peter grabbed her, encircling his arms around her. Michelle gasped. Her face was so close to Peter's she could feel his breath on her cheek. Peter held her. The terror in her eyes shocked him, and although he let her go, he just wanted to hold her until it disappeared.

Michelle trembled. She wanted to scream! To run! But... Peter's arms had felt so warm, so comforting. Never before had she felt such security. She just wanted to stay there. Michelle gave a little cry, turning away from Peter. He didn't try to stop her. She clutched her arms around her and slowly continued up the hill. Peter followed. After a minute he asked, "Did you hurt yourself?" Michelle hesitated in her step.

"No," she said, not looking at him. "Thank you for catching me."

"The walkway is a bit uneven. Maybe we should have come earlier before the sun had set." In the dusk the walkway had disappeared into the shadows cast by the buildings and trees. Peter was walking beside her now. "Are you sure you weren't hurt?"

"I'm all right," Michelle told him.

"I forgot how dark it gets once the sun falls behind the mountains," Peter said. He was afraid she would trip again and it would be his fault. "Let me take your hand. I really don't want you to fall."

Michelle stopped. Peter reached out to her. It took her a second, but sensing his sincerity she let him take her hand. For an instant she wanted to snatch it back, but something inside her wouldn't allow her to. They walked together hand-in-hand until they reached the hotel. Peter reluctantly let go when he opened the door for her. As she passed him their eyes met briefly. It was Michelle who looked away.

Chapter Ten

When Michelle got out of bed she opened her drapes but the tops of the mountains were cut off by a low cloud cover. She only stood looking for a few minutes before she went to the bathroom to prepare for the day. She couldn't help wondering what Peter had planned to do or where they would go. Peter—so different from any man she had ever known. Then—she hadn't known too many men. She had married Max the first semester of college. He was really the only man she had been close to since her father died when she was a child. As she shampooed her hair she wondered what made men so different. The memories of her father were pleasant ones. He was a hard worker and she had always felt secure with him, but he wasn't very outgoing. Max was different. She was first drawn to him because of his confident manner. It had not been easy for her to make major decisions, so it was comforting to have someone around who could make them. It was only a matter of hours after their marriage that Michelle realized she was uncomfortable with the possessive and arrogant way Max treated her. She was surprised by his actions. She didn't know how to deal with them or who to talk to about them. So, over the years it was just easier trying to guess his reasons for his actions and reactions to things she said and did. Thank goodness for her children who helped take her mind off a lot of things. Maybe she depended on them more than she should have, but she didn't feel she'd had any choice. Thankfully, they hadn't judged her or questioned her actions and affection.

Peter was a knight in shining armour coming out of nowhere to save her. Michelle found it hard to understand why he would be so kind. He hadn't made his profession known when they had met in Florence or in Switzerland, so it couldn't be duty. Even at their first meeting he seemed drawn to her and she liked him. Yes, she thought to herself as she put the last touches to her make up and as her heart skipped a beat, she really did like him.

Immediately she felt guilty. What would Max think? He'd probably try to kill Peter. He was jealous of Michelle doing anything he couldn't control. She couldn't speak to Peter even as a passing tourist. Max's touches were threatening, his words insincere, but Peter's were different. When he touched her on the arm or on the hand, she felt reassured and safe. The only frightening thing about them was her reactions. Would he change? Would he become as aggressive as Max? She was not sure, but her heart did not want to think about it. She liked how he made her feel. Was that wrong? Again she was not sure.

The knock on the door startled her. "Michelle?" Peter called. "Are you up?"

Michelle opened the door slowly. Peter took one look at her. "Are you feeling okay?" he asked noting the wary look on her face. "Didn't you sleep well?"

Did her thoughts show that clearly on her face? she wondered. "I'm fine," she told him. "I really am."

Peter liked the way she clipped back her hair so it was off her face but still hung long over her shoulders. "Are you ready for the day?"

Michelle had stepped away from him to let him into the room. "What are we doing?"

"Well, the first thing is to run down to the dining room for a good breakfast, then you'll need to check out." He stopped. "You leave from Munich tomorrow and the place I'd like to show you is just a short ride from there, so it is probably best to get a room close to the airport to stay in."

That sounded reasonable to Michelle, but her heart cried, I don't want to leave here. He was waiting for a response. As she went to get her suitcase to pack she said, "I suppose that's wise."

Peter was taken back by her hesitation. He hoped she hadn't had a bad night or that she didn't have second thoughts about going home. He didn't want to see her go but knew it was for the best. He hoped he wasn't pushing her into something she really didn't want to do. He knew she would be better off away from her husband, but were his own motives selfish? He didn't think so but he would have to watch himself and not counsel her into doing something she would eventually regret. She was still married no matter the circumstances, and he had no right to take advantage of her troubles. When he saw her come in Emergency he had just wanted to protect her, to get her away from the person who had hurt her. Now, the more time he spent with her, the more time he wanted to spend. He had grown to care for her very much.

Peter let Michelle put her few belongings in the suitcase before taking it from her. "We can leave this here till we have something to eat. We'll come back for it before we check out." Michelle could feel a bit of strain in Peter's voice but overlooked it as she tried to sound enthusiastic about the day.

"What have you planned?"

Peter got his excitement back. "I want to take you to the top of the world today. So far up you can touch the sky." He opened the door for her and waited for her to walk ahead of him down the hall. "I want you to see the view of the world from God's throne in heaven."

Michelle stopped. "Is there really such a place? I thought I had been close to God's throne when I stood on the mountain in Switzerland."

"Oh Michelle," her name was like a gentle caress. "You will be so high you can see the face of God and marvel at this world of beauty as you stand in his footsteps."

Michelle entered the elevator. "Are you kidding me?" Her mind couldn't comprehend anything that spectacular.

"I don't think so. Just you wait and see. I think you'll love it as much as I do." Peter took her into the dining room. "I've asked God to lift the clouds just for the afternoon so you can see his world through your eyes."

Michelle was speechless. All she could do was say, "Thank you, Peter."

Peter didn't dare look at her. There was something very appealing in the sweet gratitude of her words.

It was midmorning by the time the train was ready to leave Salzburg. Michelle found it very depressing to have to say good-bye to the city she now considered her sanctuary. It had been a safe haven. She couldn't help thinking as the train left the station, that she would not have this security for long. She brushed the thought out of her mind, and turned to watch the cathedral, the monastery and the rolling hills as they passed out of sight.

Two border guards checked first Peter's passport and then Michelle's even while the train was moving. They looked at Michelle, the passport, and then over to Peter. Speaking in German they exchanged a few words. Michelle only understood "Doktor." With a slight nod they gave Michelle back her passport and moved on. Peter didn't speak. He just gave Michelle a reassuring squeeze of her hand. He, however, was relieved. Some other constabulary might have asked more questions about his purpose with Michelle. Again his profession made his task of helping this woman easier. He did not mention this to Michelle.

Michelle dozed from time to time as the train sped swiftly down the track. She did not need her walkman when she was with Peter. The world around her was peaceful and his interest in doing what she wanted made it easy to be with him. She found no need to escape.

Max didn't waste time going to the police station and getting the photo of Michelle over the wires to the other Austrian towns and cities. He distributed them himself at the train station in Innsbruck. The ticket agent took one look at the photo and shook his head, but as Max turned away he asked for it back. The woman in the picture was familiar. It took him a minute to realize the photo was of the same woman he had seen struggle through bruised swollen eyes to get on the train. Yes, he told Max. This woman boarded the train several days ago to go to Salzburg. Max hurried back to the police station. That had been seven days ago. She might not be there any longer so his best bet was to have the police do the checking to save him time and money. If they found her in Salzburg, he told them, they were to watch her but not alert her that he was coming. If she was bruised like the agent said, he didn't want them asking her questions. For all they knew she had become separated from him, and he would surprise her with a visit. It would be a good reunion, he told them.

So...Max waited, pacing, drinking coffee. He was pleased when the officer at the desk called him very shortly and told him Michelle had left Salzburg and that she was on her way to Munich. Max had no idea why Michelle would go to Munich. The officer said nothing about her going with anyone else. She had picked up the ticket on her own. As Max made arrangements to fly the short distance to Munich on the earliest flight, he marvelled at how Michelle had stayed away so long. She couldn't have been hurt too badly, he told himself. Already he was imagining all the things he would do to make her pay. She wasn't so smart after all.

It was Michelle who spotted him first. The train began to slow down even before it reached the station. Michelle was surprised to see so many trains either coming or going. Just before they stopped completely she saw a tall dark man in a tweed coat with leather patches on the elbows. He had his back to the incoming train, reading the schedules of arrivals and departures on the overhead television. She didn't have to have him turn around for her to know it was him. She gasped, crunching back into her seat. Her stomach turned, her face paled.

"Michelle! What is the matter? Peter grabbed her by the hand. He was astonished at how ill she suddenly looked. "Are you in pain?"

She cowered closer to the back of the seat shaking her head. It was hard for Peter to understand what she was trying to say. "M-Max!" she gasped.

Peter looked out the window. People were leaving the train now and it took him a minute to see the face, eyes wide, mustache twitching. For a second he didn't know what to do. "I don't think he saw you. He's skimming the crowd trying to watch all the doors."

"What should I do?" she whispered as if speaking might alert Max to her whereabouts. "I don't want him to find me."

Peter leaned forward to look out the window again. Max hadn't moved. "I don't want him to find you either." Then he sat back, having a second thought. "Do you think you should face him? You know, get it over with?"

Michelle was shaking her head even before he finished asking the question. "No. No. He'd probably make me go with him."

"He can't make you," Peter reminded her.

"I'm just not ready," she told him weakly.

"I don't see any police or officials with him. He must have come by himself. Look, I have an idea. We won't stay in Munich. We'll go right on to Garmisch. It's only a two hour ride so we will have plenty of time to return here before your flight leaves tomorrow." He thought for a moment. The crowd leaving the train had thinned out and he could see Max pacing the pavement waiting and watching. "I'll keep an eye on Max to see if he tries to get on the train. Maybe he thinks you spotted him and are staying on. While I block the window you take your suitcase and carry bag and go into the toilet. Lock the door and don't come out until I knock and tell you it is safe."

"What are...?"

"I'm going to get tickets to Garmisch, but I want to be able to keep an eye on Max as well. I'm counting on his not remembering me. This train will probably leave in about fifteen minutes. Do you think you can stay calm and locked in till I return?" Peter gave Michelle a smile that gave her courage. Peter stood to block the window.

Michelle tried to be invisible as she moved past him. "What if someone wants in the bathroom?"

"They shouldn't. You're not supposed to use the toilet while the train is in the station. Just remain silent if someone tries to open the door. Think you can do that?" Michelle didn't know, but she would try. "I'll hurry," Peter said as he approached the exit with her. "Here, in you go." Michelle didn't stop to think. Her suitcase and carry-on went in first and she followed closing the door behind her. "Now lock it," he said. His tone was emphatic. Michelle slid the bolt before turning on the light. The little cubicle glowed. She closed the lid on the toilet and sat down. She looked at her watch. Fifteen minutes would be a long time. Her head suddenly ached and she wondered if she could stand it in this confined place. She tried to take deep breaths but her breathing made it harder to hear what was going on outside. Several times she thought she heard footsteps, one heavy as if a man, the other lighter, probably a woman. She couldn't tell if they were entering or leaving the train. She gulped in another breath, then listened. People were talking, but she thought they were too far away to want to try the bathroom door. Her headache seemed to subside as she tried to keep breathing. The train hissed and clanged as if someone were banging on the sides. She heard doors shut and what was probably suitcases being dragged on the pavement. Oh, please don't let him find me, she prayed. She looked at her watch. Only five minutes had passed.

Max was perplexed. Just the odd person was leaving the train now and he had not seen his wife. He pulled at his mustache as a familiar looking man stepped onto the platform. The man didn't slow down or stop. He walked directly past Max and went to the ticket counter near a magazine stand. Max was beginning to feel the anger rise. Where did the little witch go? He was sure he hadn't seen her. The Salzburg police said she had boarded this train. Where was she? Maybe, he thought returning his attention to the train. Maybe she had spotted him and stayed on. "I'll just bet...." He started toward the train. Just as he grabbed the handle to pull himself aboard, a conductor asked for his ticket. Max tried to explain to him that he did not want to go anywhere, he just wanted to get aboard. The man grabbed his arm and pointed toward the ticket booth trying to explain to him that he could not get on the train without a ticket. Max could see the people boarding the train purposely going around him and the official. "I don't want a ticket!" he yelled. "I just want to see if someone is on the train." He pulled himself from the grasp of the man and stepped inside. Immediately two uniformed policemen were upon him. That is what Peter saw as he stepped back onto the train through the entrance to Max's left. Max caught a glimpse of him out of the corner of his eye, but he was too busy trying to pull himself clear of the hands that held him to pay much attention. He finally had no choice but to step back. The policemen took him into the security wing of the station just as the train lurched ahead. He swore out loud as he saw the train and probably Michelle slip away from him.

Chapter Eleven

Michelle prayed silently as she sat on the toilet straining to hear the noises outside. It was hard to distinguish between what was in her imagination and what was real. People were passing by the door now and Michelle hoped no one would want in. Then she stood. Her heart stopped. She could hear the voice. She could make out the profanity and the anger. Max was right outside the door. Was he on the train then? Her hand was on the latch. Should she open it? Should she confront him here and now? Fear made her shake. For a few seconds she could even feel the repeated blows to her face and stomach. She let go of the handle as if it were hot. No matter how long it took, Michelle knew she would not open the door. Let the train take her to the edge of the earth—even if Peter did not get back to her. Then all went quiet. The harsh voices were gone. Michelle was so relieved she hardly felt the tug of the rail car as the train began its slow acceleration out of the station.

A tap on the door. "Michelle. Michelle."

Michelle opened the door almost falling out. She sobbed uncontrollably as Peter guided her to the seat. His arm was around her, but Michelle felt only relief. Peter let her cry, not caring what those around him were thinking. He didn't feel any need to explain. Slowly she sat up, glanced out the window to make sure Max was nowhere in sight, then relaxed against the seat. Peter withdrew his arm. She gave him an awkward confused look.

"That was close," he finally spoke.

"I could hear him," Michelle whispered her voice raspy from the tears. "W-where is he now?"

Peter gave Michelle a sly little grin. "The last time I saw him the train police were ushering him into security."

"Oh no!"

"It's all right. They thought he was trying to board the train illegally. The Germans are quite careful who comes and goes through their country. For all they know Max could have been a drug dealer out to blow someone away." He chuckled. "He'll be fine. They'll put him in a room until he cools down. Then once he tells them his story they'll let him go."

"Will he catch up to us?"

"I don't think so. He wasn't even sure you were on this train, or he may think you were able to sneak by him in the station. He didn't seem to recognize me. I made sure I walked right by him. And," he added as an afterthought, "even if he figures you are on this train he won't know where you are going. This train goes to Garmisch but it is an insignificant little town usually only visited by tourists. If he thinks you are trying to get away, he'll probably think you are on your way to Zurich, to Italy, or even back to Innsbruck. There are so many possibilities it will be days before he can track you down, and by that time you will be sitting safely in Billy's care in Montreal." He did sound reassuring, Peter told himself. He only hoped he was right.

Michelle looked at her watch. It was only ten past one. She was so weary she could hardly keep her eyes open. "It is funny how stress makes one tired." She had not realized she had said it outloud.

"It is very draining," Peter told her. The look in his eyes

was filled with concern. "You still aren't well and this just adds to the fatigue. Are you hungry?"

"I don't think so. Even if I was I don't think I want to put anything in my tummy right now. It may not stay down."

Peter slid to the aisle edge of the seat. "Here, take my jacket and use a pillow. I will wake you before we get into Garmisch."

Michelle tried to smile but it was more a grimace. Her energy was gone. It took a few minutes to fight through the maze of images before she finally was able to sink down into a fitful sleep.

It was the afternoon sunshine piercing the window that finally woke Michelle. Peter, his head back against the seat, also had his eyes closed. I'm playing him out, Michelle thought. Why does he put up with me? She watched him in his sleep. His hair really wasn't as brown as she had first thought. In fact, it was laced throughout with streaks of dark grey. She looked at him intently, wondering how old he was. She knew nothing about his family and whether he was married or single. The sun was warm on her back and she shifted in her seat to look at the scene moving at a steady speed past her window. Sometime she hoped to ask Peter about himself—if she had the courage.

"Aah, God answered my prayers. The sun has peeped through the cloud cover." Peter leaned over Michelle to look closer. There's lots more snow on these German Alps than on the Swiss ones."

Indeed there was. Michelle couldn't believe the change. Ridges of granite stood out like giant sentinels guarding the valley the train was running through. Several low-lying peaks disappeared into clouds and snow was well into the tree line.

"Beautiful aren't they?" said Peter leaning back into the seat.

"Very," Michelle said simply as she added more pictures

to her memory files. She wished she could paint so she could materialize the images once she got back home. Max had the camera, not that she knew how to use it, and she had not picked up any postcards since Innsbruck.

Soon they were standing in the station, Michelle's suitcase in Peter's hand. "I'm going to make a phone call to reserve a room, and after I store your bags we will take a little tour. We'd better go soon or it will start getting dark before we can reach heaven." Michelle followed as Peter made the call, speaking fluent German. He laughed aloud at something that was said. Funny, thought Michelle, his laughter was hearty but not boisterous. After storing the suitcase and carry-on, Peter held out his hand for Michelle to take. He didn't force it on her, he just held it out and let her make the decision. She dropped her eyes as she let him curl his fingers around hers. As they walked down the street together, it took a few minutes for her to catch her breath and feel comfortable with his hand. Inside she had to calm the battle between fear and friendliness.

Peter didn't hurry, but his pace was steady. "Frau Neuner at the guest house says the next train leaves at two. That will give us plenty of time to pick up a sausage while we wait in line. Shall we do that?" he asked as he gave her arm a little swing.

"Okay," Michelle told him.

They were eating the last mouthfuls of their Bavarian sausage, smothered with sauerkraut and rolled in a long bun, when the conductor called. Michelle had never seen such a small train. It was like a toy with room for only two people on a seat. Its wheels were that of a large caterpillar and it was so low the conductor towered above it. The train was open, its movements slow. The cool breeze felt good. Because there was only a roof and no walls, Michelle could clearly watch the mountains, trees, and trails as they crept past her. They were climbing steeply; Michelle could tell by the popping of her ears.

She swallowed hard until the congestion cleared. Peter and Michelle were in the second car close to the front of the train. "We'll climb about nine thousand feet in three miles," Peter told her. "It's such a steep grade the little cog in the middle of the train catches on the rails and keeps the train from sliding back down."

Michelle wasn't sure she felt entirely safe, but the people around them were talking and pointing, enjoying the view. You'll never do this again, she scolded herself, so sit back and enjoy it. Peter will not let anything happen to me. Michelle pushed the trickle of fear to the back of her mind and took more notice of her surroundings. Just as she was thinking they had gone really high, they levelled off and picked up a bit of speed. Something was changing as the sky began to get darker and darker, and soon their surroundings were nothing but walls. "Keep your arms inside," Peter instructed kindly. "The tunnel is a tight one and if you reached out you could touch the sides." Michelle could feel the drag and hear the sounds of the little engine as it pulled them up the mountain. It felt as though they were going straight up, but Peter explained that they were actually going up a series of switchbacks. Eerie shadows clung to the damp walls between the dim glowlights that seemed to hang on nothing.

The discomfort Michelle felt began to spread to her head, her thighs, and her bottom, but the part that hurt the most was between her shoulder blades. The little bench was solid wood with no padding and the back of it caught her right at shoulder blade level. In addition to the physical discomfort Peter now had his arm around her making her uneasy. "Are you uncomfortable, Michelle?" Peter asked as she wiggled and squirmed. "What can I do to make it better? We still have a ways to go."

Michelle leaned forward on the bench to move the pressure points to different parts of her body. "If I just didn't hurt I think I could handle the rest."

Peter moved his arm. "Did my arm make it worse?" He hoped it didn't. He liked the thought of holding her.

"I just need to move. I guess I still have some sore spots." She tried to find a more comfortable position. When she sat back she wiggled until Peter put his arm on the back of the bench.

"Stay there," he said "I don't mind you leaning on my arm." Michelle wished she could read Peter's face in the faded light.

Peter tried to take Michelle's mind off the ride by telling her about the five thousand athletes, officials, and spectators that rode this little train up this mountain many times to participate in the 1936 Winter Olympics. It wasn't just the majesty of the Zugspitze or the beauty of the village of Garmisch-Partenkirchen with its alpine chalets and pretty flowers, or even the music and gaiety of the local pubs with their kegs and beer steins, it was the people themselves. They were a noble race always trying to improve themselves and their relations with their neighbors. Peter couldn't wait till they reached the top because he knew Michelle would love it.

Peter's voice seemed to be coming through a funnel as her ears plugged and the walls slipped by like a glove sliding over a hand. It was hard not to feel as though she were being devoured by some great monster.

She sucked in a mouthful of air and found it surprisingly fresh. "You're holding your breath Michelle," Peter whispered close to her ear. "Try to take big deep breaths; there's lots of good air." Michelle did as she was told and the tightness around her lessened.

"I don't know why I feel so edgy. I'm not afraid."

"It's the change in air pressure. The oxygen is piped in and most people don't take advantage of it. If you relax and take big deep breaths, you'll feel better. It won't be too long now. It's a long way up to God's throne, but it is well worth the ride." Peter gave her shoulder a gentle squeeze and smiled. Michelle couldn't help but smile back. It wasn't just from the light comment but the touch he gave her that sent ripples of pleasure down her arm and into her heart. It was so satisfying, she couldn't be afraid.

Michelle reveled in the feeling for a second keeping her eyes averted. No way did she want Peter to see how she felt, for she was sure it showed on her face. To hide her feelings she asked, "D-does this train go down the same way it went up?"

When Michelle didn't tighten up with his touch he immediately wondered why. She wouldn't look at him but he knew she had not found his touch repulsive. He answered her question the best he could. "The train is going up the Zugspitze but I believe it comes down another mountain called Alpspitze. I'm not entirely sure. I take the train some of the time just to feel the contrast between confinement and freedom. The freedom you feel when you get to the top is exhilarating." Peter was watching for any reaction from Michelle.

"I can't wait," she told him. The tunnel then began to lighten. Streams of sunlight, almost too bright, poked through cracks in the wall. Michelle straightened trying to see ahead.

"We're not there yet." Peter explained. "When the train stops we will be in a big room but it is a cable car room. We have to take a brief two minute ride before we reach the top."

Sure enough, only a few minutes later, the train stopped and the few people aboard scurried toward the gondola. The ride was such a short one, like an elevator, that she didn't even have time to get nervous. She was too busy clearing her mind of the claustrophobic feeling of the tunnel. The cool air hit her like a wall when she stepped down from the cable car. There was a breeze and it bit at her face. Sucking in a mouthful of air sent her brain reeling. Peter was instantly beside her and she felt his arm around her. She looked up at him, but it was the scene beyond him that caught her breath. She stopped. Miles and miles, on for eternity it seemed, the mountain tops spread like a mottled blue and white carpet of peaks and ridges. Michelle exclaimed, "They are all below us."

"I told you we would be in heaven," Peter said, his arm over her shoulders to guide her to the railing. "We are above the mountain peaks, the clouds, and even the alpine skiers that come year around to ski. Look, even the bobsled and luge runs are busy." Michelle couldn't believe her eyes. It was a new world. "Look," Peter said again pointing above and around her, "there is nothing higher, only heaven. It always makes me feel grateful to be a part of all this," he gestured with a sweep of his arm, "even though I am such a small insignificant part." Michelle knew exactly what he was trying to say. She clicked on the camera in her mind and shot mental pictures of everything she could see. It was then that she saw them, not far away, but within arms length. Birds—little black birds floating on the alpine breezes. Not once did she see them move their wings. They just seemed to fall from the steep rocks and float, wings reaching to heaven catching the breath of God. Peter let her drift in her thoughts until her body began to shiver from the cold. He wrapped his arm tighter around her and held her close.

Michelle was floating in the wind beside the alpine doves: God's symbol of peace and freedom, soaring under His power not her own.

Michelle's lips were blue, quivering in the cold air. Peter hated to move, but he didn't want Michelle to catch cold. She needed a good hot meal and an early night so she could contend with tomorrow. He had a hard time even thinking about tomorrow for then she would be gone. Peter watched

Michelle, motionless except for her eyes that were following the little doves. The bruises still visible on her face were covered by wisps of hair blowing in the wind. He brushed his lips over the fluffiness just enough to savor her presence. He had no desire to let her out of his sight, but felt he had no choice.

A loud clanging bell marking the time of the last gondola down the mountain brought Michelle and Peter out of their fantasy. With Peter's arm still around her, Michelle looked up into his face. It was all he could do not to kiss her right then and there. For a second Michelle couldn't move. There was a beckoning look on Peter's face. It drew her in. She dropped her gaze and leaned her head against his chest. Peter held her for a brief moment, then let her go. "Come on love," he said not realizing he had used the endearment. "It's time to return to earth."

In her euphoria, Michelle allowed herself to be ushered into the last gondola going down the mountain. Her emotions had never been so deliciously confused. There was no fear, no feeling of imprisonment, no anxiety. She felt free, protected, and loved. What had brushed her hair? What had Peter called her? What was happening to her? How could she feel so different? Right now she did not want to try to sort it out, it was too fulfilling.

The gondola ride down was far from frightening. Michelle stood with the others watching the mountains change from rugged granite rock crevices and glaciers filled with snow to thick green forest. Michelle's eye caught the flight of another kind of bird and she knew it was a great soaring eagle. He used his wings to lift himself above the tree tops, then soar on the wind before diving to the earth. She did not feel the jerk of the gondola as it stopped or sense that her feet were on the ground as Peter walked her toward the streets of Garmisch-Parten-Kirchen. Michelle had no sense of reality. She was flying with the eagles.

Max sat in the train station watching the train disappear out of sight. The police had confiscated his passport, put him in the security room, and left. There was no use of his trying to leave. He knew those doors locked behind them. He would just have to wait until they returned. What a waste of time. Michelle was probably laughing at him if she had been on that train. Somehow, he was sure she had seen him. Maybe he should have been more discreet, hiding behind a pillar or partition or something. He was so angry he just wanted to hit something or some one. He began to pace twisting the corner of his mustache as was his habit. *That woman,* he cursed going to the window to watch other trains come and go. *What was she trying to do to him? How much did she think he could take?*

Two men in dark blue, nearly black-colored uniforms came in sometime later. They didn't seem to be in any hurry but they did give Max back his passport. They told him to sit, and though he preferred to stand and holler obscenities at them for making him miss that train, he knew from experience that they wouldn't let him go until they were sure he would not cause another disturbance. They wouldn't have returned his passport if they thought he was a threat to their country. No. He would have to play their game, and if he was lucky he would be allowed to circulate flyers and watch the trains. They might even help him in his search.

Max took a seat across the table and in a more civil tone began to explain his actions. He didn't apologize or justify them. In his mind they had been warranted, but he had to speak civilly enough to get their support. Several hours had passed by the time he left the terminal. After explaining his need to find his dear lost wife, he received their approval to search for her. Max picked up his luggage from where he had stored it. He felt quite sure that Michelle, if she was on that train, was long gone. He wanted to believe she was just running around the country until it was time for them to leave from Frankfurt. He wanted to believe this but suspected this was not the case. She had some childish bee in her bonnet and he had no idea what she was up to or where she was going. He would get a room close to the station and come back to hunt her down. There was just over a week left before his plane left and he would not stop searching until he had her. How long he would stay in Munich he did not know, probably just until the German police spotted her somewhere else. She couldn't hide forever. Tomorrow he would have more flyers, and Max was sure he would find her with the help of the efficient German officers.

Chapter Twelve

Frau Neuner met Peter and Michelle as they entered Neuner Gastehaus. "Herein! Herein! Doktor Zimmer!" She bustled around the desk to grasp Peter by the hand and pump it.

Peter greeted her with "wie geht es ihen?" He gave her a friendly kiss on both cheeks and turned to Michelle. "This is Michelle," he said to Frau Neuner.

"Aah! Aah!" She gave Michelle an approving look and called, "Alfonse! Dokter Zimmer." A balding little man with sagging cheeks and a twinkle sparkling in his eye hurried into the room wiping his hands on a towel. "Guten Tag, Peter," he said giving Peter a hand shake. "It is nice to have you return," he said in English.

"It is nice to be here Herr Neuner. I want you to meet Michelle." The reverie Michelle experienced on the street was gone and she eyed these friendly people with apprehension. The hugs and kisses were something she was not used to and it was hard not to let her discomfort show. She gave them her most sincere smile.

Frau Neuner said something to her husband, who left the room quickly, and she led the way up the stairs. Opening the door to the first room at the top, she swung it wide so Michelle could enter. The room was spacious with a wooden framed bed and a wash basin and pitcher sitting on a matching bureau. The wall paper on two of the walls was a profusion of tiny red flowers with small green leaves. The thick duvet on the bed had the same floral cover. The curtains on the window were a creamy color tied back with a floral band to match the rest. A blind had been closed for the evening. "For you," Frau Neuner said in simple English, and then she spoke to Peter.

Peter put Michelle's suitcase on a chair. "The bathroom is at the end of the hallway. It's just us tonight so we won't have to share it with anyone else," he said.

Frau Neuner was already out the door bantering Peter to follow. "I'll be right back," he told Michelle following their hostess to his room. He was back in a minute.

Peter came in without wearing his jacket. "Alfonse has dinner waiting so we'd better go down. Are you up to potato cakes and cabbage rolls?"

"I am hungry," Michelle said removing her coat.

Peter and Michelle were alone in the dining room. Michelle, sitting across from Peter could not bring herself to look at him. Her emotions were too sharp and she was afraid they would show. She didn't know if it was because of the close encounter with Max, being suspended in time on the Zugspitze, soaring over the mountains, or just sitting around the fire in a cozy warm atmosphere with someone she felt safe with. Her feelings were so intense they were almost tangible.

Frau Neuner spread the meal before them and left. They ate, mostly without conversation, but the atmosphere between them was not one of strain but of melancholy. They both knew their worlds would change tomorrow.

Michelle loved the glowing fire in the big open hearth that sat in the middle of the room. The few dining tables were on a floor two steps above the canopied fire, which was encircled by a cloth padded bench.

"Let's have our dessert down by the fire," Peter suggested when Michelle had laid down her fork. He slid back his chair and went down the stairs first. "I love coming here," he said as if speaking to himself. "Especially when I have the place to myself after tourist season and before skiing." He took a seat on the bench sliding into the flickering shadows to make room for Michelle.

Frau Neuner was hesitant in bringing the desserts and coffee but when she looked in on the pair sitting by the fire, she sensed by the distance between them that it was probably a good time. She didn't know what the situation was between Peter and this woman. She had noticed the yellowish brown bruise on Michelle's chin and too much darkness around her eye to be makeup. She didn't want to make judgments on what Peter was up to because she knew in time he would tell her.

"The cake is too much," Michelle told Peter. "Do you want to eat it."

Peter laughed lightly. "No, I'm stuffed with cabbage rolls."

"It was a lovely meal." Michelle watched the flames bounce as the fire crackled and snapped.

"I think I'll wait till later to have coffee. Do you want yours now?" Peter sat up as if to take the pot from the tray and pour.

"No, I'll have mine later as well." Michelle lay her head back giving her hair a little shake.

She sure is beautiful, Peter thought. I wonder when my feelings for her changed from caring to loving? He covered up his thoughts by saying, "I really don't feel like going back to work." He said this but his heart was really saying, *I want to stay here with you forever.*

"I wish I could take all this with me. I don't know if I can leave it behind." In Michelle's heart she was crying, *I don't know if I can leave you.*

There was a heavy silence, then Peter slid closer to Michelle. He could not let this chance slip away. It was getting late but he didn't want the night to end. Carefully he slipped his arm around her and slowly drew her close. This time he could feel her tighten, but he didn't let her go. Still gazing into the fire Peter said, as softly and sincerely as he could so she wouldn't pull away, "I wish you weren't going." There! It was out! His feelings for her were now said. Peter could feel her strain against his hold and he almost released her. "Michelle, I can't let you go without you knowing how I feel." He kept his voice low. "Please? I-I know I haven't any right...." Michelle turned slightly, lifting her head as if to speak. Her brown eyes, her tiny nose, the color on her chin....He lowered his head and placed a feathery kiss on the bruise. She was wide-eyed when he looked at her but she did not pull away. Her bottom lip quivered, and he tenderly covered it with his. She gave a little gasp, then returned the kiss.

It was a fleeting embrace. Michelle could feel the fire through her whole being—a frightening fire, but she did not want Peter to let her go. The only sound in the room was the crackling of the flame. Peter took Michelle's hand in his but didn't take his eyes off the flickering colors. He rubbed his thumb on the back of her hand, and she shivered. He wanted to kiss her again, but he knew that would only frighten her as a heavy footstep would frighten a little alpine dove.

Slowly she began to relax and let the light touch send ripples up her arm. Michelle slid closer and leaned her body against Peter. It was so easy to rest her head on his shoulder. She would not fall asleep. There were too many questions in her heart.

It took her a long time to speak for fear the magic of the night would be gone. "Peter?" her voice a whisper. "What am I going to do without you?"

"I guess the same thing I am going to do without you—hope and pray."

"Hope and pray?"

"I hope and pray that sometime in the future we will be together."

"I love you, Peter." Michelle didn't move.

Peter pulled her to him and held her to his heart. "I suppose it is only natural for you to think you love me. I don't doubt that you do. I only wish we could see into the future to know what will become of that love. Did I get too close, too soon? Did I take advantage of your situation? Right now, my love..." he stroked her hair, "I think we both need to do some thinking. You need to sort out your life knowing I will be there if you need me. However if you find that your life is with Max, I will understand. It's you I love and I only want to see you safe and happy, even if I am not part of that life." Michelle didn't know what to say. She just wanted to stay in his arms, but that little voice inside told her he was right. "You are so important to me Michelle," Peter continued as he held her. "You brought a love to me that I have not had for many years. I really do hope you are a part of my future but if you aren't, you have given me back the knowledge that I can love again." Michelle didn't quite understand but right now she didn't care. She just wanted to be held.

Max was out of the hotel early. He stopped at the police station to pick up the flyers being printed. He left a few with the officers, the others he took. Back at the Munich station he paced, sat, drank coffee, and talked to many people leaving the trains. He had permission to search the platforms but he was not allowed on the trains. That was up to the officials. This angered Max for fear Michelle would spot him and hide. He had to wrestle with his emotions to stop from striking out at something or someone. Several times before noon he phoned the police station but no one had any word as to his wife's whereabouts. Michelle's disappearance bothered Max more and more. She not only had left and made him look like a fool, but she had actually planned and carried out an escape. From the money, to the passport, to involving the children, she must have planned this even before she left Canada. He had to give her credit, she was good. What a sucker he had been! He was so angry, he smashed his coffee cup onto the table spilling its contents onto his pants.

Michelle slept well even though she didn't think she would. As she lay under the snuggly warmth of the duvet, she couldn't imagine herself away from Peter. She wanted to spend as much time with him as she could, and they didn't have to leave for Munich until twelve forty five. They would take a taxi from the train station to the airport where she would board the plane just before the flight. They had stood together while Michelle phoned Billy to tell him of her plans. Billy said he had spoken with Sonja but he did not tell his sister that Michelle was coming to him. He didn't think it wise they know until she was actually there.

When Peter said goodnight to her the night before, he told her he wanted to take her to a few shops in Garmisch before they left in the morning. They would have a snack at Frau Neuner's and say their good-byes to her and her husband and then get on the train. She hurried to wash and get dressed. Their day would go fast enough.

Peter was having coffee with Alphonse while he waited for Michelle. He could hear her moving around upstairs and hoped she'd had a good night. He told Alfonse about Michelle and how he was trying to get her out of the country before her husband caught up with her. He was very nervous about getting out of the train in Munich. He was sure Max would be watching. "Why wouldn't he go look somewhere else?" Alfonse asked. Peter said he figured Max would have the police everywhere so he wouldn't have to run around. "I really believe Max will be at the station and I'm not sure how to handle that. I just have to get Michelle from the train to the taxi then I think we are in the clear."

"I will wish you luck," Alfonse said as he stood when he saw Michelle descend the stairs.

Peter and Michelle had a lovely morning even though the day was dull with a high overcast of clouds, but the mountains were still clear under the grey ceiling. Michelle pulled her coat tighter in the coolness and let Peter take her to several little shops. A couple of times he seemed preoccupied, but when she questioned him he denied any problem. They were walking by a little shop of children's toys when Peter brightened. "Do you like teddy bears?"

Michelle was surprised. "Cute little things I can cuddle."

"Come on," he said and opened the shop door for her. "I want you to pick out a large bear, a really large bear, one that is definitely not you, like that one," he said pointing to a big brown bear dressed in Alpine attire.

Michelle laughed. "That definitely is not me."

Peter took it down off the shelf. "He's kind of cute: vest, hat with feather, even the leather pants. Look, it says Zugspitze on his vest. What a nice souvenir! You must have him!" His voice was getting higher the more he talked.

"Peter!" Michelle hadn't seen him like this before.

Peter calmed down. "I'm sorry," he said setting the bear on the counter. "I didn't mean to raise my voice. It's j-just..." He took Michelle to a corner near a shelf of books away from other customers. He didn't go without the bear. Michelle saw his face grow serious. "I think you should take the bear. He may save your life and get you out of the train station."

"H-how?"

"If Max is watching the trains or the airport, and I suspect he is, you will have a hard time getting to the taxi or plane without him seeing you. With Bear here, you may have a chance. You can get off the train holding the bear high so he can't see your face. We will dress you in a German coat, one of the beautiful furs, and if we walk together, with me between him and you, we might just get away with it. You're hair could be a problem, but if you wear a hat maybe he won't notice."

She had almost forgotten about Max. She just thought he'd be gone by now and she wouldn't have to worry.

"He may not be there," Peter added, "and if he isn't then you'll have a big souvenir of Germany." Michelle agreed. Peter told her he was paying for these few things so she'd have money when she got home.

In the train they had two hours to talk. Peter went over the plan one more time then let the matter rest. They talked about Michelle's children, of her likes and dislikes. Together they laughed as Peter told her of some of his hospital experiences. When he got to the part of his European excursions, that is when Michelle decided to ask him about his family. The Zugspitze bear sat on the edge of the seat while Michelle and Peter, both dressed like Germans, talked. Sometimes Peter would even hold her hand.

Michelle no longer flinched at his touch. "Peter, last night you said I had brought love back to you. Does that mean...?"

"I was married a long time ago." His tone reflective, almost monotone. "I was still in medical school, she was an intern at the same hospital. We were terribly in love. I could hardly study. Just a little while after we were married, nearly a year..." he paused, "Amy was diagnosed with cancer. It was a hard six months; I just wanted to take the pain away. Here we were around the best doctors and they could not make her better."

Michelle could feel the sadness in his voice. "And you never married again?"

"For a long time I didn't think I needed anything more than Amy's memory. After many years I decided I didn't want to be alone, so I began dating." He took both her hands in his. "It wasn't until I saw you in Florence that I thought my search was over. Then I found out you were married." His tone dropped. "I was devastated. It was a sheer coincidence when I saw you in Switzerland, but when I saw you lying on the stretcher in the hospital..."

"Peter." Michelle placed her lips on his. No one on the train seemed to care.

The train pulled into the Munich station all too soon. Peter put his emotions aside and took over. He had Michelle lean back in her seat while he made a visual tour of the station platform. It was a busy day for Saturday because of the soccer teams in town but, "that could be an asset," he told Michelle. He looked for Max as people began exiting their car. Then he saw him shoving and pushing closer and closer to their exit. It was almost as if he knew where they were sitting. Peter took Michelle in one hand, the bear clutched to her, and her suitcase in the other. He had Michelle's carry-on bag on his shoulder. His stuff he had left in Garmisch. Instead of going forward he started for the back door. It was a little tight going against the flow but he only hoped Max did not notice. He stuck his head out. Max was watching every door the best he could. When Max glanced in the opposite direction Peter pulled Michelle from the car and struck a straight line to the other side of the building, Bear held high against her face. Though the taxis to the airport were close to the train, so was Max. Peter raced Michelle across the station and out a far door. It may take a bit longer to get to the airport but Peter wanted to evade Max at all costs.

Max watched the doors intently. He was frustrated. Another day was ending and he still had not seen his wife. He looked for Michelle's coat in the crowd, her long hair, her suitcase. He watched for someone skulking around or a girl in a big hurry. Lots of people carried souvenirs, from walking sticks to cuddly bears. Just look at that monstrosity. Who would ever want a bear that big? The couple were making a straight line for the main exit, the man pulling the woman as if he had a purpose. Max went back to watching the train hoping he hadn't missed Michelle while he was gawking at that ugly bear. As he saw the thinning crowd he wondered why the bear had attracted his attention. The woman must have been European; her clothes appeared to be, anyway. And the guy. He stopped. That guy was familiar. Somewhere he had seen those leather pants, the high top green socks, the alpine hat with the feather, and the suitcase. Before he had time for second thoughts, he knew the woman was Michelle. Off and running he went, faster and faster to the main exit. He was breathless by the time he saw them getting into the taxi. He was hollering when the taxi pulled away.

Michelle collapsed into the back seat. Immediately Peter put his arm around her and held her. "I don't ever want to treat you like that again, but I was scared."

"It's all right," Michelle tried to console him as he took a glance out of the back window. He saw Max as he waved and shouted on the sidewalk. Peter held Michelle until they were out of sight. Slowly he sat back, looked at his watch and told the taxi driver to take an alternate route to the airport. He didn't want to arrive until boarding time.

Max flew back into the station, momentarily confused. He glanced up at the train schedule for no reason and a thought struck him. He grabbed a cab and told the driver to get to the airport as fast as he could.

Peter and Michelle said their good-bye's in the car. Peter knew timing was a big factor. They arrived just as a voice called for passengers to board Flight 541. Again Bear stayed close by while they hurried. Michelle already had her ticket in her hand. Her luggage was small so she would carry it with her. They scurried through the metal detector and down the long hallway. The attendant only looked briefly at Peter's identification and at the urgency on his face and let him pass through security. "I'll be right back," he assured.

They ran up the hall and under the canopy of the plane entrance. A voice was announcing the final call when Michelle reached her seat. Peter put her suitcase in an over-head compartment and handed her the carry-on bag. Bear still sat on Michelle's lap as he leaned over her. "I think we made it," he told her, his breath on her cheek. "Please call me as soon as you can, you have my numbers." He kissed her soundly and turned to leave. "I love you," were the final words he spoke.

"I love you too, Peter," she said but he was already gone.

Max ran into the airport letting the taxi wait. The over-head departure board was flashing Flight 541 to Montreal. Cursing, he looked around. There was an open door across the terminal concourse. A luggage train carrying large crates was moving under a grey roll-up door. Max paid no heed to the security guards standing at either side of the door. All he saw was sunlight. Michelle was on her way to Billy and he had to stop her. He made a bee-line for the door just as it started to roll down...

Peter left the jet-way thanking the attendant for letting him take Michelle to her seat. He just wanted to run, not to see the plane take Michelle away. But, he couldn't bear to see her leave so easily. On the observation level he watched the push-back vehicle hook up, the refuelling pumpers leave, and the wing-walkers make sure all was clear. The boarding canopy receded; the jet way bridge contracted; the strobe light under the wing flashed its farewell. Then the A340 Airbus backed up taking Michelle out of his life. How his heart ached.

The plane continued to back up and then turned to face the open runway. Peter could hear the engines roaring and in his mind's eye envisioned Michelle waving at him. He gave a little wave back as he started to turn away. A black haired man with a black mustache ran out onto the runway from an open baggage door, two security guards chasing, hollering something Peter could not hear. Other people in the observation concourse also saw the chase and in every language began to chatter and point. Everyone was at the window now.

Max was pleased to see the plane still sitting. He had made it past the guards and through the open door. He was running as fast as he could yelling the only words he knew to stop a plane. "Bomb! Bomb!"

The guards stopped. The wild man was screaming something but the jet thrust from the engine drowned out the words. The wing-walkers, heading back to the terminal, caught sight of Max racing around the blast wall, flailing his arms. They started toward him and stopped! The Airbus roared. Max was lifted off his feet as the breakaway blast pummeled him into the cement wall like a piece of fragile china.

Peter stood aghast, both hands on the window glass.

Waving their batons and pointing them to the ground, the wing-walkers rushed back to the plane inching its way down the runway. The plane stopped. As Peter ran to the security station, emergency vehicles scurried to the inert body lying at the base of the cement wall.

Michelle's heart jumped. They had stopped. Max! Somehow he had stopped the plane. A cry escaped her lips. Her eyes darted back and forth. Max is going to get her. *Oh, Peter*, her heart cried. She buried her head in her hands and waited. The pilot announced over the speaker a technical problem and all passengers were to leave the plane as quickly as possible. "The plane will not return to the terminal so please be careful on the stairs down to the runway." Leaving all but her purse, her feet as heavy as her heart, Michelle followed the stewardess.

As she stepped down to the tarmac she expected Max to grab her any second. She was so dejected she had to keep her eyes to the ground for fear people would see her tears. She paid no attention to the activity or chatter around her. All she could do was think about Max and how futile her life was.

"Michelle?" Michelle stopped. The voice was gentle, the touch on her hand tender. "Michelle?"

"Peter!" Michelle exclaimed, her heart skipping a beat. "You stopped the plane!"

Peter wrapped his arm around Michelle turning her slightly to see the activity near the blast wall. "No, Max did." He pulled her closer and walked into the terminal. "Come on, my little Alpine Dove. I'm taking you home."

Judy Ann Crawford

Biography

Judy, a freelance writer, is a regular columnist in the Taber Times and has published articles and short stories in a variety of publications including, ProLife Magazine, Alberta Scoutlook, Arizona Senior World (Gilbert, Arizona, USA), Lethbridge Living Magazine, and others.

She is a creative writing instructor for Taber Adult Learning Council and Brooks District Further Education Councils, and for numerous writing groups, and does readings in the local schools.

A Business Management graduate of Brooks Campus, Medicine Hat College, Judy has also taken a Writing Fiction course from Independent Study BYU, and is a graduate of Quality of Course Writing School in Ottawa, Ontario, Canada.

Currently Judy is a member of the Oldman River Writers of Lethbridge, Alberta, the Writers Guild of Alberta, the Canadian Authors Association, and the Lethbridge Children's Literature Roundtable.

A mother of five sons and one daughter, Judy currently resides in Taber, Alberta, Canada, where she has taken up writing as a full-time career.

Judy is also the author of the acclaimed novel *A Place for Troy*.